Jake Stellar
The Obedience of Fools

Jake Stellar
The Obedience of Fools

By

Rodney Riesel

Published by Island Holiday Publishing
East Greenbush, NY

ISBN: 978-0-9971149-3-5

First Edition

Special thanks to:

Pamela Guerriere

Kevin Cook

Cover and book design by:

Connie Fitsik

To learn about my other books friend me at

https://www.facebook.com/rodneyriesel

For Brenda,
Kayleigh, Ethan
& Peyton

Chapter One

It was Sunday afternoon and hotter than hell. Bree had to work and I was bored, so I went into the station to do some paper work I had been putting off for far too long. I glanced back at the door behind me; CAPTAIN MERLE STEIN, the glass insert read. The door was closed, locked, and the lights were off. Merle had told me, when I spoke with him the night before, that he might stop down. But he hadn't made a showing, and I was the only one in the room.

I had turned on the television that sat on a three-quarter-inch plywood shelf across the room just for the noise, and even made a pot of coffee. I hadn't gotten back up to pour a cup yet, but it sure smelled good.

The television was tuned to ESPN. Grinning like an idiot, I watched Jacoby Ellsbury round the bases after hitting one into the bleachers for a three-run homer against Boston. Watching him loop from base to base I remembered back to a time when I hated Ellsbury. It's funny how much better a man becomes when he slips into the pinstripes. Bree and I had lived in North Myrtle Beach for over ten years now, but we were originally from the Bronx and my loyalty still remained with the team I grew up watching on TV and whose home games my father took me to on Sunday afternoons.

I got up from my chair and walked over to the coffee maker. I poured myself a cup, and as I took my first few sips, I lifted the lid of the Krispy Kreme box that sat on the table in front of me. I knew the donuts were at least two days old, but I took one and bit into it just the same. It was a little stale and the glaze had become a bit crunchy, but I hadn't eaten lunch yet, and just about anything would have tasted good at that point. In my book, even a stale Krispy Kreme beat the hell out of Dunkin Donuts any day of the week.

I knew I shouldn't be eating donuts; I had recently put on a few pounds. I hadn't run much through the winter, or even the spring. It's easy to slide right back into bad habits.

I sat back at my desk and dotted some I's and crossed some T's, as they say, and then signed my name, Detective Jake Stellar, to the bottom of each page. Next to my signature, I filled in the date. I stacked the pages neatly and slid them into a bin on the corner of my desk.

I leaned back in my chair and put my feet up on the desk. I sipped my coffee, took another bite of my crusty old donut, and stared at the television.

It was the bottom of the eighth and the score was tied at 6-6 when something caught my attention out of the corner of my eye. I glanced over at the door to see Captain Stein unlocking it. The door entered into the detective's room and wasn't used by civilians. We were supposed to keep it locked at all times, and sometimes we did.

"Working hard, or hardly working?" he asked upon entering.

I always hated that line. Everyone seems to say it

with that *ain't-I-so-clever* tone of voice, as if they coined the phrase themselves and were the first person to ever utter it.

"Good one," I said, as he walked on by me and unlocked his office door. "You make that up yourself?"

Merle ignored my jab and looked at the on duty board that hung on the wall next to the door that led to the lounge. "You see Perkins?" he asked.

"Nope."

"How long you been here?"

I glanced up at the wall clock. "About three hours."

"Bree working today?"

"Yup. Till four."

Merle flipped on the light in his office. Then I could hear him opening and closing drawers and doors. I reached over and grabbed the remote control off of my desk and turned up the volume a little to drown out the noise.

"Am I bothering you?" Merle asked.

"A little." I gulped down the remainder of my coffee and sat the cup back on my desk. "Lose something?" I asked.

"*Lose* something suggests that I originally *had* something." He slammed a drawer.

"What are you looking for?"

"Paperwork that needs to be filled out before Lint comes back to work."

Oh yeah, I remembered. My partner, Avis Lint, was returning to work tomorrow. It had been almost seven months since he was shot in the shoulder as we attempted to serve an arrest warrant up at Lake Moultrie. Recovery doesn't usually take that long, but an infection took hold and didn't want to let go.

I pulled open the bottom drawer of my desk. "They're right here in my desk," I informed Merle.

I heard another door slam and he shouted back, "What the hell are they doing in *your* drawer?"

"They've been here for over a year."

"That's right," he recalled, as he walked into the squad room. "Ever since *you* were injured in the line of duty."

Injured, Merle made it sound as though I stubbed my toe or got a hangnail. I wanted to remind him *I was stabbed for chrissakes*, but I let it go.

Merle reached into the drawer and grabbed one of the copies.

"Take them all," I said.

"No, now that I know where they are, I'll be able to find them next time."

"That's what you said last time, and hopefully there won't be a next time."

Just then Officer Pat Murray stuck his head into the squad room from the hall that led to the front desk. "Jake, an exterminator just found a body in a room over at the Ocean Bay Club."

I stood, opened my top desk drawer, and retrieved my pistol; a Smith and Wesson .45 semi-automatic. "Male or female?" I asked, as I holstered my weapon.

"Don't know yet. The bug zapper didn't speak English all too good and he hung up before the dispatcher got all of the information. Two units are en route."

Didn't speak English all too good. I let it pass: after all, I don't speak English all too good most times either. As I made my way for the door I heard Merle say, "I'll ride along, Jake. Pat, you hunt down Perkins and have him meet us there."

"Roger that, Captain," Murray responded.

Chapter Two

I parked my truck on the first floor of the parking garage at the Ocean Bay Club. Two patrol cars were already there; one parked in the street with lights flashing and the other in the garage. An emergency vehicle from the North Myrtle Beach Fire Department and an ambulance were also parked half in the street and half on the sidewalk.

Merle and I took the elevator up to the twelfth floor. When the doors parted, we walked around the corner and onto a walkway. As we walked along, the doors to each condo were on our left; to our right was a railing and a forty-foot drop to the roof of the parking garage. I glanced over the edge; Merle didn't. It was obvious he didn't like being up that high, so I nudged him toward the railing with my shoulder. He almost shit himself.

"Jesus Christ, don't do that!" he hollered.

I chuckled. "Falling never killed anyone. It's the sudden stop at the end that gets ya."

"Very funny."

An officer was speaking with an elderly woman at the door of unit 1208. I heard her say, "Sorry, officer, but I don't hear too good these days," as I walked by.

We came to unit 1209; a uniform was standing near the front door. I nodded, he nodded back, and I went in. Merle followed.

The door entered into a hallway that led to the kitchen. As we walked into the hall I glanced back at the door knob and then the strike plate. *No evidence of forced entry*, I thought. Lying on the floor were three pairs of running shoes, two pairs of women's and one pair of men's.

A bar with three bar stools separated the kitchen from the dining room, and the dining room opened up into the living room. There were four bedrooms; three off the hall and the master off of the living room. All of the beds were made.

The body of a man in his mid to late thirties lay on his stomach in the middle of the living room floor, next to the coffee table. His feet were pointing toward the dining room with his head pointing toward the sliding glass door. His head was turned to his left. The sliding glass door was open and led out on to a balcony.

I stood over the body and Merle walked out onto the balcony. The victim was wearing running shoes. He was dressed in a blue T-shirt with the sleeves cut off and a pair of red gym shorts. His hair was cut very short. His legs and arms were muscular, but not bulky.

One of the firefighters said, "Detective."

"I looked up. "Yeah?"

"We're gonna take off. Doesn't look like we're needed here."

"Yeah, thanks guys."

The firefighters nodded to the ambulance crew, who

were also in the kitchen. "Catch you guys later," one of them said. Talking shop and their evening plans, they made a noisy exodus from the building.

I knelt down next to the body. Knowing Crime Scene hadn't been here yet, I was careful not to touch or disturb anything. There was a large bloody gash on the victims left temple and a bullet hole—an exit wound—in his back, between his shoulder blades. There wasn't a lot of blood on his back; most of it was on the carpet beneath him. I glanced at the walls for a bullet hole but didn't see one. I stood and looked around the room for what may have caused the dent in the victim's head.

Merle walked back into the room followed by another uniform I knew as Conrad Barns. They were commenting on the view from the balcony—not the ocean view, but the bikini clad ladies twelve stories below, lounging tantalizingly around the pool.

"No weapons found?" I asked Conrad.

"Not even a pea shooter," he responded glibly.

I looked around the floor. "The subject picked up his shell casings."

Conrad shrugged. "So he's probably done this before."

"Or he watches a lot of television," I offered.

Merle bent down and picked up a lace doily from the coffee table, and with it, he picked up a mermaid bookend that sat on a shelf in the entertainment stand. Keeping the doily between his fingertips and the bookend, he showed it to me. There was blood on its base.

"Well, I guess we know what caused the gash in this guy's head," he said.

My attention went back to Conrad. "We know who the victim is?"

"I sent Pierce over to the rental office to get some information. It's right across the street."

Tom Powers walked through the door. "What do we have here, gentlemen?" he asked.

Thomas Powers was with the Horry County Coroner's Office. He was wearing a red Hawaiian shirt and jeans and he carried his medical bag. It wasn't often we beat him to the scene.

"Nice shirt," I said.

"I was hosting a cookout at my place."

"Sounds fun."

"I *was* having fun, but now I'm here."

"The victims a male," I explained. "Mid to late thirties. Took a single gunshot to the torso and a bookend to the side of the head."

Merle held up the bookend—the torso of the comely mermaid whose long hair covered the good parts. The companion bookend was the mermaid's coiled tail. Both were cast iron and potentially deadly when not used for their intended purpose.

"Huh," Tom said. "I have those same mermaid bookends at home. I guess I better hide them the next time Gale gets mad at me."

Gale was Tom's wife. She was one of those wives that made everyone ask, "How the hell did he end up with her?" She was five-eight, thin, blond, and looked like a supermodel. He was barely over five feet and reminded me of a miniature Richie Cunningham on class picture day. I guess some hot chicks just naturally go for that aw shucks, clean-cut type. Or maybe Tom was just the anatomically correct male doll she'd always wanted. Tom was about thirty-one but looked twenty-one. Gale was in her mid-twenties.

Merle glanced back at Conrad. "Evidence bag," he said. "I'm not going to stand here and hold this thing all day."

"Oh, sorry, Captain," Conrad said, and hurried over to the bar and grabbed one of the larger clear plastic bags lying there.

Merle placed the bookend inside the bag, zipped it closed, and sat it on the coffee table.

Tom Powers grabbed the victim by the shoulder and rolled him onto his side. "Bullet entered through the abdomen and exited through the back."

I looked up at the ceiling. "There it is," I remarked. I grabbed one of the dining room chairs, slid it over underneath the small hole in the ceiling, and climbed up. "Grab one of those bags, Con." Conrad snatched up another bag and held it open directly beneath the hole. I reached into my pocket and pulled out my truck keys. With the tip of my key, I pried the bullet loose and it dropped into the bag.

"Two points," Conrad announced.

Tom gently rolled the body back to the way it was and then unzipped his medical bag. He looked over his shoulder toward the ambulance crew. "Let's get a gurney and a body bag up here."

"You got it," one of them answered, and the two of them trotted down the hall.

I jumped off of the chair and went into the master bedroom. There was an open suitcase on a chair. Inside the suitcase was a pair of tan cargo shorts and a few men's shirts. An empty suitcase sat on the floor in the closet. Two sun dresses and a bunch of women's tops were hanging from the closet rod above the suitcase. Next to the suitcase were several pairs of women's shoes.

On top of a mirrored dresser were a few one-dollar bills and some change. Also lying there were two racing bibs, numbers 564 and 565. I walked back into the living room. "Okay, let's get Crime Scene in here to dust for prints, get some blood samples, and take some pictures," I said.

Chapter Three

It was four o'clock by the time I got home; Bree would be home any minute. I walked from the garage into the kitchen and then into the living room. The dog was sound asleep on a blanket that Bree had laid on the couch that morning.

"What's up Woofie?" I asked the dog. She didn't move, so I said "Hey!" a little louder. She raised her head, opened one eye, and gave me an annoyed look. "I said, what's up?" She dropped her head back on the blanket. "Okay."

I walked over, picked up her water dish, filled it, and placed it back on the pink mat that Bree had recently ordered—because, apparently, every dog's dishes need to be on a thirty-dollar custom mat with their name stitched on it.

I then went to the fridge in search of the left over pizza I knew was waiting for me. We had ordered it the night before from Lucky's Pizza, in my opinion, the greatest pizza on the Grand Strand. I pulled back the plastic wrap, removed three pieces, and placed them on another plate. I set the slices to nuke for one minute and grabbed a ginger ale.

Ding! I grabbed the plate and went into the living room. I sat in my chair and reached for the remote. Suddenly, with a plate of food on my lap, the dog was now interested in me. I lifted my plate and Woofie jumped into my lap.

"I bet you're here for the pizza," I said. I sat the plate on the arm of the chair, picked up a slice, and took a bite. Woofie's head went back and forth from the pizza to me like she was watching a tennis match. I tore off a piece of pepperoni and fed it to her. It went down so fast she never tasted it. I gave her another small piece.

Just then Bree walked through the door; I heard her car keys hit the counter top. Woofie jumped from my lap and ran to Bree. "Not quite the welcome I got," I mumbled.

"There's my baby girl," Bree said in a childish voice. "Mommy loves her baby."

Bree walked into the living room holding the dog. I was halfway through my second slice of pizza. She glanced down at my plate.

"Is that your dinner?" Bree asked.

"No," I answered. "It's my snack before dinner."

"You're just dying to put more of that weight back on, aren't you?"

I folded the rest of the slice and shoved it into my mouth. "We can't all have a body like you."

"You weren't feeding the dog pepperoni, were you?"

"No." I figured the dog wouldn't narc on me. It doesn't take them long to learn not to bite the hand that feeds them.

"If her breath smells like pizza you're in trouble."

"Her breath probably smells like her own ass."

Bree shook her head and left the room. "Let's get Woofie a treat."

"What did you want to do for dinner?" I called out.

She didn't answer. All I could hear from the other room was, "Sit … sit … sit and I'll give you the treat. Sit … sit."

I knew the little rat didn't sit, but the next thing I heard was her crunching on the treat. After all these months it was obvious that the dog thought *sit* meant to just stand there and stare at us with her head cocked, because she got a treat every time she performed that command.

"What did you want to do for dinner?" I repeated, this time with a bite of my third slice of pizza in my mouth.

"When will you be ready to eat again?" Bree asked.

"Whenever you are."

"Don't you want to wait a couple hours?"

"I didn't eat lunch today. I was starving when I got home. Geez, get off me about the pizza."

"I'm just picking on you. Calm down."

I picked up the remote and began surfing. I stopped when I got to an old episode of CSI: Miami. David Caruso's acting style always kills me. It's like watching a leprechaun trying to be macho

Bree returned to the living room, still holding the dog. She sat on the couch and put her feet up. Woofie jumped onto her blanket and curled up next to her. "I'm going to lay here for a half hour or so, then I'll get ready. Where did you want to eat?"

"Wherever you want?"

"I'll eat anything."

"Here we go again," I mumbled. I pulled the handle of my recliner and laid back.

"What was that?"

"Nothing."

*****

It was after six o'clock when I opened my eyes. Bree was still sound asleep, and so was ratdog. I picked up the remote and lowered the volume on the TV. Bree opened her eyes.

"Hey," I said.

"Hey," she replied.

"Did you want to get ready and go grab something to eat?"

"Not really. You want to have something delivered?"

"Sure. What do you want?"

"I'll eat anything."

"*Ugh*. Chinese?"

She turned up her nose. "Nah."

"Subs?"

"No."

"We had pizza last night."

"I know. Just get Chinese."

Getting up from my chair had lately become a chore; the longer I sat, the harder it was. If it had a built-in toilet, I'd probably never get up. "They should rename these things Fat La-Z Bastards," I sighed to myself, and went into the kitchen in search of a take-out menu. "What do you want?" I called out from the kitchen.

"The usual."

The usual was pork fried rice, sweet and sour chicken, chicken and broccoli, and a shrimp egg roll. I made the call to Hong Kong Chinese Restaurant and placed the order. They said it would be here in forty minutes.

When I returned to my recliner Bree asked, "How was your day, did you get a lot of paperwork done?"

"Not really. Mostly I watched the game and then we got a call."

"*We*?" she asked.

"Merle stopped in just before we got the call; he rode over with me."

"Where did it happen?"

"Ocean Bay Club."

"Tourist?"

"Not exactly. It was a guy by the name of Roger Truitt. He and his wife own a condo there. They spend six months here and six months in Westerville, Ohio—a suburb of Columbus. They're both retired."

"How old was he?"

"He was only forty-four; looked a lot younger, though. According to the wife, he started some Internet company—don't know exactly what it was, yet—and it was bought out for a bunch of money a few years ago."

"Must be nice … don't look at me like that, you know

25

what I mean. Is the wife okay?"

"Yeah, she wasn't there. Another couple is staying with them. The Truitts and the other couple took separate cars and drove over to Tanger Outlet. According to Marnie—that's the wife—Roger forgot his wallet and drove back to the condo."

"Was it a burglary?" Bree asked.

"Doesn't seem to be. Mrs. Truitt looked around the place, she didn't notice anything missing."

"That's horrible," Bree said, shaking her head. "At least she has friends there. That's good, she doesn't have to be alone."

"The worst part is, they were supposed to leave Friday morning, but Mrs. Truitt wanted to stay to run the 10k here in town this morning."

"So she's blaming herself."

"Exactly."

Bree sat there silent for a few seconds and if I know Bree, and I do, she would think about that poor woman losing her husband for days. Makes me wonder why she even asks about things like that. She carefully got up from the couch, trying not to disturb the sleeping ratdog, and said, "I'm going to jump in the shower before the food gets here."

"You want some company?" I asked, already knowing the answer.

"Nope."

Bree was halfway down the hall when Woofie jumped off the couch and followed her.

"She doesn't want any company, dog," I called out.

"Don't listen to Daddy," Bree assured the dog with that damn baby talk. "Mommy *wuvs* Woofie's company,"

Chapter Four

I slammed my truck door and walked into the North Myrtle Beach Police Department. Ah, Mondays, nothin' like 'em. A lot of Mondays I don't know what to expect when I walk through that door. This Monday, however, I did know. First of all, Lint was back; second, there was yesterday's homicide to investigate.

The second I saw Avis Lint sitting at his desk with that huge grin on his huge face I wondered if we were supposed to do something for his return. Should we have bought him a cake? Should we gather around him and pat him on the back and say, "Hey old buddy, glad to have you back?"

No sooner did I finish that thought when I heard the door open behind me. It was Detective Gwen Lawrence; she was holding a cake. *Fantastic!* Now I won't have to listen to him bitch all day about no one caring.

Gwen walked past me and sat the cake on Lint's desk; his smile grew to twice its original size.

Perkins walked out of the lounge and up to Lint's

desk. He slapped Lint on the back and said, "Hey, old buddy, glad to have you back."

Shit. I was going to use that line.

Gwen bent and kissed Lint on the cheek. "Nice to have you back," she said.

Wow, a little overboard, don't ya think? Then I realized I had the expression on my face that went right along with what I was thinking, so I smiled real big and said, "Yeah, Lint, the place just wasn't the same without you." It wasn't a lie. It was quieter, and the donuts didn't disappear as fast.

"Thanks, Jake," said Lint. "It's nice to be back. Now get a knife, this cake ain't gonna eat itself."

Perkins grabbed a few small paper plates from the stack that sat next to the coffee maker and handed one to each of us as Gwen cut into the cake.

Captain Stein's door opened. "Oh, yeah," he commented when he saw the cake. "Just in time for the party."

Gwen placed a small wedge of double chocolate layer cake on a plate and handed it to Merle. "Here ya go, Cap'n." Rank has its perks.

Merle gobbled up his piece quicker than any of us, crumpled the plate in his hand, and said, "That was good—now get to work everybody."

"Did we get the coroner's report back yet?" I asked.

"No," Merle answered. "I guess they're pretty backed up. Powers assured me he would get to the autopsy around one this afternoon."

I glanced up at the clock and then at Perkins. "Where is Marnie Truitt staying?"

"Two floors down—1008. Some friends of her and

her husband's own the condo and aren't using it this week. Mrs. Truitt and her guests are staying there until Crime Scene clears her place."

"When will that be?"

"Some time this afternoon, I'm told."

"Come on, Lint, shove that cake in your head and let's get going," I said as I headed toward my desk to retrieve my weapon.

As he got to his feet Lint sliced another piece and loaded that one into the old pork trap as well. I swear I heard one of the stitches in his shirt pop.

I holstered my .45 and together Lint and I walked out to the parking lot. I made my way toward a shiny, black, brand-spanking-new Dodge Charger.

"What?" Lint asked. "When the hell did we get that?" He walked around the unmarked cruiser with his mouth agape. "This is awesome!"

"You're damn right it is," I said, opening the driver's side door. The new car smell made me euphoric. I'd read somewhere the distinctive odor came from volatile organic compounds that might be toxic. Who cares, at least I'd die happy. "We got it last week."

Lint held up his hand thinking I would just toss him the keys. "I want to drive," he informed me.

"Ain't gonna happen," I informed him.

"Why?"

"Because I'm driving."

"But I usually drive."

"And now you're not. Now shut up and get in."

Lint climbed into the passenger seat with a groan. "Holy shit. How do they expect us to climb in and out of this thing quickly?"

"What do you mean, *us*? And anyway, when have you ever done anything *quickly*?"

I slid into the driver's seat with ease. "See, nothing to it."

"It looks like there is more room in the driver's seat. I could probably get in and out a little easier if you let me drive."

I pulled the door closed. I loved the red-blooded *thunk* it made. "I guess we'll never know."

"That's horse shit. I always drove the other car."

"The other car was a Taurus, and besides, you didn't *always* drive. You drove sometimes."

"What does it matter that the old car was a Taurus and this one is a Charger?"

"If you don't know, you shouldn't be allowed to drive it."

"I'm just saying, it would probably be a lot more comfortable for me in the driver's seat."

"Maybe if you limited yourself to one piece of cake for breakfast, the *passenger* seat would be more comfortable." I started the engine, gave the gas pedal a couple pumps just to make sure Lint knew what he was missing, and then roared out of the parking lot.

"Enough with the weight jokes. I'll have you know, I lost ten pounds in the last few months."

I pointed at Lint's belly. "I think I just found 'em, they're hanging over your seat belt, there."

"Ha-ha, very funny."

I took a left onto North Kings Highway. We made it almost two blocks before Lint said, "So what did you want to do for lunch?" Two blocks was a new record. Maybe he had turned over a new leaf. Probably to see if there was a donut under it.

Chapter Five

We parked on the fourth floor of the parking garage and took the elevator up to the tenth floor of the Ocean Bay Club. Heights didn't seem to bother Lint, like they did Merle, so I opted not to push him toward the railing; it probably wouldn't have supported his weight anyway. And no one would believe it was an accident.

I knocked on the door of unit 1008. A darkly tanned man in his early forties wearing navy-blue shorts, a beige Polo shirt, and blue and white striped boat shoes answered the door. I introduced myself, and then Lint. The man introduced himself as Brock Carmichael. I asked if we might come in and have a word with Mrs. Truitt. He sighed and ran his perfectly manicured fingernails through his bleach-blond hair as though now wasn't a good time, but said, "Yes, detectives, right this way."

"Thank you," I said, and we followed him down the hall to the living room. The floor plan of 1008 was exactly the same as 1208. The only difference in the condo was the paint, flooring, and furniture ... and no one was lying face down dead in the living room.

"If you gentlemen would like to have a seat I'll go and get Marnie."

There were two striped chairs on the north wall of the living room that seemed to match Brock Carmichael's shoes. I took a seat in one of them and Lint sat in the other. A matching sofa stood against the south wall across from us. In front of the sofa was a glass-top coffee table.

Carmichael walked down the hall and lightly tapped on a bedroom door. "Marnie," he called out in a loud whisper. "There's two detectives here to speak with you."

I heard a woman reply, "Tell them I'll be right out. See if they would like a cup of coffee."

Carmichael returned to the living room and told us what she said, but he didn't offer the coffee. From the looks of him I just assumed he considered himself far too high up the social ladder to serve coffee to two lowly police detectives. I thought about offering *him* a cup, but I was afraid he might accept, and then the day might end with me carrying his golf bag around the country club while Lint washed his balls.

I turned my head and stared out the sliding glass door at the ocean for a second and when I turned back, Lint was reaching into a candy dish and grabbing a Reese's Peanut Butter Cup. With surgical precision he unwrapped the foil, removed the paper, and popped it in his mouth. I wondered how many of them he would eat between now and when we left. I also wondered how old they were.

The bedroom door at the end of the hallway opened and out walked a tall, barefoot brunette. She wore black yoga pants that said AB-FREAK down one leg, and a black tank top that exposed her belly. When I glanced down at her abdomen I could tell right away she was definitely an ab freak, and I didn't even know what that was. She slowly walked down the hall toward us, placing one foot directly in front of the other, like a runway model showing off the latest fashion in workout wear. I figured she was wearing all black because she was in mourning. I stood and then glanced down at Lint; his jaw was hanging open, which reminded me to close my own.

I stood, Lint didn't; I suspected the pudgy bastard was nursing a boner. "I'm Detective Jake Stellar with the North Myrtle Beach Police Department, and this is Detective Avis Lint," I said, offering my hand.

She took my hand and gave it a slight shake. "Jake Stellar. Wasn't there an old 80s cop-show called *Jake Stellar*?"

Jesus H. Christ, if I had a dollar for every time somebody asked me that, I'd be richer than Donald Trump says he is. "Not that I'm aware of, ma'am."

"Please, call me Marnie." She sat in the center of the sofa with her legs pulled up under her perfectly sculpted butt.

Lint was still staring. I thought about snapping my fingers in front of his face but that would be a little too obvious, and besides, she was probably used to the stares. So instead, I grabbed another peanut butter cup and tossed it to him. It worked as well as tossing ball of yarn to a cat.

Carmichael was now leaning against the bar watching us. He had made himself a drink, a double shot of whiskey on the rocks. I knew it was whiskey before I even saw it, because I could smell it, and that amber color was unmistakable. It's been over eight years since I took my last drink but every time I smell it I want it. Someone once told me that that feeling goes away eventually. That person lied. I wanted a drink now just as bad as I did the day after I quit.

"Marnie, you told the officers yesterday that you didn't notice anything missing from the condo. Is that correct?" I asked.

"Yes … I mean, I quickly looked around. I didn't notice anything missing."

"Your original plan was to leave Friday morning?" Lint asked.

"Yes," Marnie replied. Her eyes slowly drifted toward the glass door. "It was my idea to stay. I wanted to run the race yesterday." It was obvious she regretted her decision.

"Did all of you run in the race?" Lint asked.

"All of us?"

Lint made a gesture toward Carmichael. "You, your husband, and the Carmichaels."

"Yes, all four of us ran."

Carmichael said nothing.

"Marnie, can you think of anyone who may have wanted to harm your husband?" I asked.

"We don't really know that many people down here. We're only here a few months out of the year and we spend most of our time on the beach, or shopping and going out to dinner."

"Did Mr. Truitt seem unusually stressed, or agitated recently?" I asked.

"No, not that I noticed. He's been his usual self."

Lint glanced back at Carmichael. "Where is *Mrs.* Carmichael this morning?"

"Bambi? Why do you ask?" Carmichael responded. He sipped his drink.

"Just curious."

"She ran to the store to pick up a few things. We didn't know how long it would be before we were allowed back upstairs."

"What do you do for a living, Mr. Carmichael?" Lint wanted to know.

"What does that matter?"

"It doesn't. Just curious."

"I'm between jobs right now, if you must know."

We asked a few more questions over the next half hour or so. Mrs. Truitt answered her questions without hesitation. Most of Mr. Carmichael's questions were answered with, "Why do you want to know that," or "Why does that matter?" Mrs. Carmichael never made a showing.

Marnie Truitt walked us to the door and held it open as we walked out. When I crossed the threshold I turned back toward her. "How was your time?" I asked.

"My time?"

"The race. How did you do?"

"Oh … good, I guess. Not my best, but not my worst."

"And Mr. Carmichael?"

"Good, I guess. I can't remember his exact time. He doesn't run as much as the rest of us."

Lint and I walked around the corner and stepped onto the elevator. I hit the number four button. When the door closed Lint turned to me and said, "I wish they had killed Brock Carmichael instead. Seems like a real douche."

I had to agree.

Chapter Six

I took a left onto Main Street and proceeded onto the Robert Edge Parkway. I caught a glimpse of Lint rotating his left shoulder and rubbing it with his other hand.

"How's the shoulder?" I asked.

"Good overall, sometimes it just aches. I didn't think it would still hurt after six months. Just getting old, I guess."

"You and me both," I agreed. "I was beginning to wonder if you were coming back at all."

"Yeah, I just needed some more time. Getting shot like that was something I never really expected. Spending a few months with Bertie up at her camp was just what the doctor ordered."

Roberta Clodfelter—Bertie to her friends—was Lint's latest squeeze. Roberta was a couple years older than Lint but looked a few years younger. For her age she looked pretty good and was sexy as hell, and she acted the part. She was a very nice woman and treated Lint like gold, something he wasn't used to. Roberta's husband had died a few years early leaving her pretty well off.

"I bet. That's some camp. Those two weekends we came up were nice; it was hard to tear ourselves away."

"I hear ya. She usually closes it up for the winter but figured it would be nicer for me to recoup up there."

"That girl takes good care of you."

"She sure does, Jake. It's crazy, I've never felt like this about any woman."

"None of your three wives?"

Lint chuckled. "Not one. I feel like a kid again, for chrissakes."

"That's great, Lint."

"The sex is—"

"Let me stop you right there, Lint. I don't really want to hear about the sex."

"Oh, okay." Lint didn't speak for a few seconds and then said, "Mary Ann stayed with us for four days when she came to visit. She and Bertie got along great. They even went to an antique show together up in Marion. Can't wait for the other kids to meet her."

Mary Ann was Lint's oldest daughter, I think, from his first or second wife, I can't remember. Lint had been married three times and had at least one child with each wife. He didn't see his kids a lot. Each time he got divorced the ex would move out of state and take the kids with her.

Lint was quiet the rest of the drive into Conway. He just stared out the window. I figured he was thinking about Bertie. I was happy for him, but I kept that to myself.

I took a right off of Main Street into the parking lot of the Horry County Coroner's Office and parked. We went into the building and asked for Tom Powers. He rounded the corner, dressed in a crisp, bright-white lab coat that appeared to be brand new, just as I said his name. I'm not that tall but I'm about ten inches taller than Tom Powers. Today he reminded me of a mad scientist who'd accidentally stepped into his miniaturization machine.

"Hey, my favorite detective," said Tom.

"I bet you say that to all the detectives." I shaded my eyes. "New lab coat?"

Powers glanced down at the coat and picked at a piece of fuzz. "Brand new."

"What about me?" Lint asked.

"What about you, what?" asked Tom.

"Aren't I one of your favorite detectives?"

"No. Now, what brings you two gentlemen—and I use the term loosely—up our way?"

"I was hoping you had finished the Truitt autopsy," I answered.

"I did." Tom walked around behind the desk and started flipping through some file folders. When he got to the one that read "Roger Truitt" on the tab, he yanked it out and opened it.

"The bullet killed him. It entered under the rib cage, severed the pulmonary artery, and exited between the shoulder blades, shattering the T-2 and T-1 on its way out. He was dead before he hit the floor."

"What about the bookend to the side of the head?" Lint asked.

"I'm guessing that was done pre-mortem, during the struggle. The victim had skin under his nails—probably his assailant's. I assume the attacker was knocked to the floor before pulling his weapon and firing, which accounts for the bullet's angle of trajectory."

"So we're not looking for a killer that's two feet tall," I joked.

"No."

"Then that eliminates you, Powers," said Lint.

"Fuck you, Lint, ya fat bastard," Powers returned. He closed the folder and handed it to me. "Everything is in there. If you have any questions just give me a call." Tom turned around and headed down the hall.

On the way back to the car Lint caught me grinning.

"What are you smiling about?" he asked.

"That eliminates you, Powers. Holy shit, did you see the look on his face? Classic."

"Yeah, now I'm surely not his favorite detective."

"I guess not." I opened the car door and got in.

"Who the hell does he think he is? *Well, if it isn't my favorite detective*. Walking around in that brand new lab coat like he's so important. I bet he bought it at Baby Gap."

We laughed about that all the way back to the station.

Chapter Seven

On the way back to the department we stopped at Sonic. Lint only had *one* hot dog and a *small* Coke—no fries. Dating Roberta Clodfelter seemed to be having a positive effect on him. A fat Avis Lint was bad enough, I would imagine a thin one would be unbearable. At least fat he provided some comic relief to the day-to-day grind. I figured if he lost any more weight I would just mention that he was looking a little too thin. Sure, that would be a prickish thing to do, but I can't ride around all day with a thin Lint. *Ha-ha, thin Lint; sounds like a Girl Scout cookie.*

I tossed the coroner's report on my desk and stuck my weapon in the top drawer. Lint made his way directly to the coffee pot. *Yes,* I thought. *He's going for a donut.* I knew he wouldn't let me down. I secretly watched as he poured the coffee and added creamer. He reached for a sugar packet, paused for a second, and then tossed it back in the basket. *Dammit!* He glanced down at the half-eaten box of Krispy Kremes, and then walked to his desk. *What the hell? It's like living in Bizzaro World.*

He placed the cup of coffee on his desk and then stowed his gun in his top desk drawer. He glanced over at me. "What?" he asked.

"What, what?" I returned.

"You're staring at me."

"No I'm not."

"Yes you were."

"It's your imagination."

He stared back at me for a second with a sheepish grin. "You missed me those six months didn't you?"

"Um … yeah, that's it."

"I figured." Lint sat down at his desk. "Don't worry, buddy, I'm here to stay. You're gonna have to put up with me for a lonnng time."

"Thank God."

"So, what's next?"

"First I want you to look into Brock and Bambi Carmichael. I want to know who they are, why he's between jobs, and why he thinks he's so goddamn important."

"You got it."

"When you're finished with that, I want you to find out who did the timing for the 10k they ran. If they used a timing chip, I want to know when they all started and when they all finished."

"Okey-doke," Lint said, and then began punching keys on his keyboard with his fat kielbasa fingers as he stared intently into the monitor.

I got up, walked across the room, and poured myself a cup of coffee. I looked back over my shoulder at Lint, and then picked up a donut and took a bite. "Oh, these are good. You want a donut, buddy?"

He looked up from his computer. "No thanks, Jake. Tryin' to cut down on the sweets."

Dammit, I just called him buddy for no reason. "Suit yourself." I wished I hadn't taken the donut, which was beginning to grow a beard, but I ate it anyway. That sure backfired.

"It was a company by the name of Tru-Time," Lint said.

"Get a call into them, see if they can give us the information we're looking for."

Merle's door swung open. "Jake, domestic disturbance call just came in from the Ocean Bay Club, condo 1008—Marnie Truitt's place. A unit is on its way."

I jumped up and grabbed my weapon. "Come on, Lint."

"Can I drive?"

"No."

We were out the door and en route in less than a minute. I hit the sirens and lights.

I could have parked on the ground level and ridden the elevator up ten floors, but I thought it would be more fun to take the Charger up to the top of the parking garage. The tires squealed around the corners as we ascended the ramps. Lint held onto the safety strap the entire way, his smile never leaving his face. When we reached the garage roof I slammed on the brakes and spun the wheel a hard right, sliding sideways to a stop.

We both leapt from the car and ran to the entrance door like Batman and Robin arriving at the office of Commissioner Gordon. Lint hit the up button on the elevator and we waited.

"That was awesome!" said Lint. "You gotta let me drive that thing."

"It's not a toy," I replied.

"Of course it's a toy. A big boy toy."

"That you'll never play with."

The doors parted and we stepped onto the elevator. When they parted again we were on the tenth floor.

We arrived at the front door of 1008; the door was propped open. As we walked down the hall, one of the officers—Pat Murray—turned. "Hey, Jake. Hey, Avis."

"Hey, Pat. What do we got?" I whispered.

"Near as I can tell, one of the women came home and caught her husband with the other woman," he replied.

"In the sack?" Lint asked.

"I don't think so."

I walked past Pat and Lint followed. There was a lamp on the floor, broken, and a frying pan was lying on the floor in front of the sliding glass door. There was a crack in one of the glass panels from top to bottom.

Officer Ronnie Pierce stood in the middle of the living room. Marnie Truitt and Bambi Carmichael were standing on opposite sides of him. They both were red-faced and looked as if they had been crying. Brock Carmichael was leaning against the bar in almost the exact same spot as when we were there last. He looked as though the commotion was having no effect on him other than pure entertainment.

"Mrs. Truitt," I said. Pierce turned around and both ladies looked over at me. "Mrs. Truitt can we step outside for a second?"

"Jake," she said, and sidestepped toward me, keeping her eyes on Bambi.

Bambi lunged toward her but was stopped by Officer Pierce. "Calm down, calm down," he said, holding her by the shoulders.

Out of the corner of my eye I could see the smirk on Brock's face.

I took Marnie's elbow and guided her outside. I turned to Lint as I went by him and said, "Talk to Mrs. Carmichael, get her side of the story."

"Roger that," Lint responded.

I closed the door behind us and leaned back against the railing. There wasn't a cloud in the sky and the sun was making me squint. I wished I had stayed inside and made Lint go outside. I also wished I hadn't left my sunglasses lying on my desk.

"So, what happened?" I asked.

"Bambi came in and saw Brock rubbing my shoulders," she answered.

"Is that all he was rubbing?"

"What a crass and unprofessional remark."

"*Mea culpa*, I'll rephrase my question, Mrs. Truitt. Was there any intimacy involved?"

"What are you trying to say? I just lost my husband yesterday."

"I'm not accusing you, Mrs. Truitt," I assured her.

"You shouldn't be accusing Brock, either."

"Were Brock and your husband friends?"

"Of course. We were all friends."

"Were?"

"Are. We are all friends."

"You're all friends *now*, Mrs, Truitt. What I meant

47

was, who was friends first? Were you and Mrs. Carmichael friends and *then* your husbands became friends, or was it the other way around?"

"Bambi and I were friends first, we met at a club … a book club."

"And your husbands met through you."

"Yes."

"Other than walking in on you today, does Mrs. Carmichael have any other reason to assume there could be something going on between you and Mr. Carmichael?"

"She has no reason to assume anything. I simply mentioned that I hadn't slept well last night and that my shoulders and neck were stiff. Brock innocently offered to rub my shoulders, and that's when Bambi walked in. I tried to explain but she started screaming at us and throwing things."

I opened the door and motioned for Marnie to enter ahead of me. When the two of us returned to the living room, the frying pan had been picked up and placed on the bar. Brock was no longer in the room.

Bambi turned toward Marnie. She seemed much calmer than when we had walked out.

"I'm sorry, Marnie," Bambi said.

Marnie put out her arms and moved toward her friend. "I'm sorry, too, Bambi."

The women hugged and Bambi kissed Marnie on the cheek.

"So, are you two ladies going to be okay?" Pat Murray asked.

Marnie shook her head yes.

"And I assume no one wants to press charges?" Lint said.

Bambi and Marnie both shook their heads no.

Pat clapped his hands together. "Okay then. Let's get out of here, Ronnie."

As Pat and Ronnie left the condo, I asked "So, we're good then?"

"Yes, Jake. Everything is going to be fine," Marnie assured me.

Lint started for the door and then spun around. He reached in the candy dish and grabbed another Reese's. "Ladies," he said, as he unwrapped the candy on his way out the door.

We got back on the elevator and I turned to Lint. "Did Murray say who called the cops?"

"Yeah. A resident on the ninth floor. Unit 9009."

I hit the number nine button.

We made our way down the walkway of the ninth floor and stopped when we reached unit 9009. I knocked on the door and reached for my badge.

An elfin woman with battleship-gray hair opened the door. She looked to be in her seventies. "Yes?" she asked.

I flashed my shield. "I'm Detective Jake Stellar, and this is Detective Avis Lint. We're with the North Myrtle Beach Police Department."

She didn't even look at the badge. "Is this about all the commotion upstairs?" she asked.

"Yes, ma'am. We were wondering if we could come in and ask you a few questions."

She pulled the door open all the way. "Yes. Come in. I was just making Myron and me a sandwich for lunch. You boys hungry? I can fix you something."

"No thank you, Mrs—"

"Penobscot," the old woman told me. "That old fart in the chair over there watching Bonanza is Myron and I'm Harriet."

The old man didn't turn around. I don't know if he didn't hear us or if what Hoss and Little Joe were doing was just a hell of a lot more important to him.

Harriet placed the top slice of bread over the bologna and cut the sandwich in half.

"I understand you called 911 about a disturbance upstairs," I said. The volume on the TV was so loud, I almost had to shout.

"That's right," Harriet answered. "Myron told me to mind my own business, and I did at first, but they just went on and on. Myron had told me what happened a couple days ago, down by the pool, and I didn't want someone to get hurt." She placed the sandwich on a plate and then poured Myron a glass of milk.

"What happened at the pool?" Lint asked.

"Those two men were arguing."

"Mr. Truitt and Mr. Carmichael?" I asked.

"Yes."

I took out my notepad and scanned my notes. "You didn't mention it to the officers when they questioned you yesterday," I said.

"No. Myron didn't tell me about it until last night, and he wasn't here when the officers took my statement."

"What were they arguing about?" Lint asked.

Harriet walked into the living room and sat the sandwich and milk on the coffee table in front of her husband. "Myron, tell these men about the argument between Brock and his friend."

Myron glanced up with a surprised look on his face.

His eyes focused on me. "Who the hell are you?" he asked.

"Myron, they've been here for ten minutes now. If you would turn off that GD idiot box you might know what's going on around you. This is Detective Lint and Detective Rockford. They've come to ask us some questions about the Truitts."

"It's Detective Stellar," I corrected.

Harriet chuckled. "Oh, I'm sorry. I knew it was the same as one of those old TV shows. Now tell them about the argument the other day, Myron."

"About the recyclables?" Myron asked.

Harriett shook her head. "Not *our* argument, ya old fool, the argument between Mr. Truitt and the guy who's been staying with them."

Myron took a bite of his sandwich. "Oh, *that* argument."

We patiently waited while Myron took a sip of his milk, another bite of his sandwich, and a second drink of milk. He laid the sandwich back on the plate, grabbed the remote control off of the end table, and turned down the volume on the television.

"It was Saturday afternoon," Myron began. "I was sitting down by the pool in a lounge chair, taking in some sun. My doctor back in Maine says us Northerners don't get enough sunlight. He put me on this pill—vitamin D. He says they've linked some forms of cancer to lack of vita—"

"Myron!" Harriet scolded. "These gentlemen didn't come here to listen to your medical history. Get on with the story."

"Where was I?" Myron asked.

"You don't get enough vitamin D," Lint answered.

"Before that," said Myron.

"The argument," I said.

"Oh yeah. Harriet says you can put newspapers in the recycling bin. I say ya can't."

"Not that argument," I reminded him. "The argument between Mr. Truitt and Mr. Carmichael,"

"Oh yeah, that's right. So I'm sitting there in the lounge chair and I see Truitt and Carmichael come around the corner, they're walking toward the beach. When they get up on that wooden bridge thing that goes over the sand dune and sea oats, Carmichael grabs him by the shoulder and spins him around. Truitt shoves him back against the railing and jabs his finger right in Carmichael's face and says, 'If you can't follow the rules, you're out. One more time and you're dead.' Truitt turns and keeps heading toward the beach and Carmichael turns around and goes back inside."

"Did either one of them see you sitting there?" Lint asked.

"I don't think so."

"Did you see them together much, other than that day?" I asked.

"Shit yeah. All the time. We see all four of them walking on the beach, sitting by the pool, even saw them out to dinner a few times."

"You ever see *just* the two men together?"

Myron thought for a second. "Did see the two of them in the gym one morning. I went down to walk on the treadmill. They didn't speak to each other much that day."

"How long have you known the Truitts?" Lint asked.

"Four or five years, I guess," Harriet answered. "We're here from January till the end of May. I believe they come down from November to May, or something like that."

"First time we ever met the Carmichael's though," Myron added. "As far as I know, they've never come down with them before."

"They been here the whole time?" Lint asked.

"No, no. They got here some time the first of April," Harriet replied.

I looked at Lint and he gave me a slight shrug. "Okay, Mr. and Mrs. Penobscot, thank you for your help. We'll leave you to your lunch."

Harriet walked us to the door. We weren't even halfway down the hall when I heard Myron crank up the television to 11.

"You boys have a nice day," Harriet called out as we made our way toward the elevator.

We walked out onto the top floor of the parking garage and Lint turned to me and said, "Nice old couple."

"Yup."

"Is that true about the vitamin D?"

I looked up at the sun. "I don't think that's anything we have to worry about here."

"You're probably right," Lint agreed. "What about the newspapers?"

I opened my door and got in. "What newspapers?"

"You can put them in with the recyclables, right?"

"Yeah, I guess." I started the engine and drove down the ramp. "You have any questions about the case?"

"Yeah. What did Truitt mean when he said if you can't follow the rules, you're dead, and what were they arguing about to begin with?"

"I wonder. And do you think he had more in mind than just rubbing Mrs. Truitt's back?"

Lint chuckled. "I had more in mind just hearing about it."

I drove down Ocean Boulevard and took a left onto Main Street.

"Jake?" Lint asked.

"Yeah?"

"One more question."

"What?"

"How many calories you think are in those little Reese's Peanut Butter Cups?"

Chapter Eight

I arrived home a little after six that evening and for the first time since we got that little dog, it met me at the door. I could say it had no effect on me, but I would be lying.

"Were you waiting for Daddy?" I asked, in that same stupid voice Bree uses when she talks to the dog.

Woofie danced around in a circle on her hind legs. She was actually excited to see me. I walked over and grabbed the box of treats off the top of the fridge.

Bree entered the kitchen from the hall. "I just gave her a treat," she said.

"You can never have too many treats," I told her, shoving my hand in the box and pulling out one of Milk-Bone's idea of a marrow-filled bone. "Sit."

Woofie sat.

"Good girl, good girl. Did you see that, Bree? She sat. Good girl."

I held out the treat and the dog snatched it from my fingertips.

Bree was smirking. "I told you that dog would grow on you."

"Yeah, like a fungus," I joked. I unclipped my holster and placed my gun in the cupboard over the range hood. "How was your day?" Bree was an RN at Grand Strand Medical Center and had her share of harrowing work days.

"Good. Pretty slow, actually. There was a one car accident out on Highway 22. The driver came in with minor injuries. The passenger was fine. How about you?" Bree bent down and scratched the dog on the head. "Did you sit for Daddy?"

She had lapsed into baby talk again. I ignored it and said, "Nothing too exciting."

"Make any progress in yesterday's homicide?"

I removed my belt and untucked my shirt. "No, but we did get called back there today."

"Oh yeah? How come?"

"How about if I jump in the shower and then tell you about it over dinner?"

"Sounds good. Where did you want to eat?"

"Duffy's?"

"Sounds good to me." Bree picked up the dog and went into the living room. "Let's watch some TV while Daddy is in the shower."

I started down the hall. "Don't call me Daddy."

"I just heard you call yourself Daddy," Bree shot back.

"Yeah, well, that's between me and the rat dog."

*****

Bree usually likes to sit outside at one of the picnic tables to people watch and catch some rays, whenever we dine at Duffy Street Seafood Shack, but today she chose to sit inside. Duffy's was a favorite haunt of ours for its un-fancy, delicious fare and rustic chic décor.

I asked, "Shall we sit at the bar?"

"No," she replied. "Let's get a table."

"Good evening, Stellars," said Lisa, the waitress, as she handed us our menus. "What can I get you to drink, Bree?"

"I'm going to have a margarita, on the rocks."

"And ginger ale for you, Jake?"

"I think I'll just have water."

"Water it is," said Lisa. "I'll grab those drinks and give you a minute to look at the menu."

"Thanks, Lisa," I said.

I don't know why I opened my menu; I already had the whole thing memorized. I had eaten here so many times I could probably wait tables—one table at a time, of course. I ran my finger down the menu and stopped when I got to my-can't-go-wrong usual; there was no need to consider anything else.

"What are you getting?" Bree asked.

"What else? The blackened fish tacos," I replied. "What are you getting?"

"I'm not sure yet."

Lisa returned with our drinks. "Have you decided?"

"Yup," I said.

"I need a few more minutes," Bree informed her.

"The new menu throwing you?" I asked.

Bree looked at the front cover. "Is it new?"

"No," I responded.

"Smart-ass," she shot back. "I'll have the clam strips, Lisa."

"And I will have the blackened fish tacos."

We handed our menus back and Lisa disappeared into the kitchen.

I sipped my water. Bree sipped her margarita. I wished I had a margarita … with a double shot … hold the margarita mix.

A basket of peanuts sat in the center of the table. I reached in and grabbed a handful. Blues played over the speakers.

"So, any leads in the investigation?" Bree asked.

Any leads in the investigation? I could take her right here on the table when she uses that sexy talk. "No, but there's a guy we're looking at."

"What's so special about him?"

"A witness overheard an argument between him and the victim the day before he was murdered. Also, the guy's wife walked in on him giving the deceased's wife a massage."

"That sounds fishy."

"That's what we thought. They both claimed it was innocent."

"But the wife didn't think so."

"No. She got into a screaming match and threw a few pans. The downstairs neighbor called 911."

Bree was sitting with her back to the front of the restaurant and something outside caught my eye. I stared over her shoulder, out the window.

"What's the matter?" Bree asked, and turned to see what I was looking at.

"Well, speak of the devil."

Brock Carmichael was standing in front of the Pirate's Cove Bar and Grill speaking with a woman. I got up from the table. "I'll be right back."

"*Really*, Jake?"

"It'll just be a second."

I walked up to the window to get a better look. I would have gone outside but I didn't want him to see me just yet.

Brock was leaning against the building, his left hand supporting his weight, and his legs were crossed. I didn't see a photographer anywhere, but I was sure Brock thought he was in a GQ photo shoot—or maybe JQ: Jerks Quarterly. He wore a pink Polo shirt tucked into his white shorts. He had on beige flip-flops, and a cream-colored sweater, tied loosely at the neck, hung around his shoulders. He looked like every spoiled rich kid in those 1980's John Hughes films. I bet if I had a dollar for every time Brock Carmichael said, "Do you know who my father is?" I could retire.

The young blond he was speaking with was at least fifteen years younger than him, and from the smiles and laughter coming from her, Brock was also one of the funniest comedians alive. I made a mental note to have him tell me a few jokes the next time we saw each other. I could always use a laugh.

The young woman handed Brock her cell phone. He began putting his number in her contacts.

I pulled open the door and shouted, "Brock! Brock Carmichael!"

He looked over, so I waved. He gave a half wave and a big grin. He didn't recognize me from across the street, but he loved that someone was shouting his name.

I stepped out onto the sidewalk and let the door shut behind me. "It's Detective Stellar!" I shouted. The smile left his face and he quickly handed the girl's phone back to her. "Hey, I was wondering if you could stop by the police station tomorrow morning around ten. We have a few more questions to ask you."

Everyone seated in front of Duffy's and the few people walking by looked on as though they were also waiting for his answer. The young lady turned and walked back inside the Pirates Cove.

"If you don't have a ride," I called out, "I can send a patrol car to pick you up."

"I'll be there," Brock yelled back angrily. He turned and walked around the corner toward the Ocean Bay Club.

When I returned to my seat, my plate was waiting for me. "I was setting up an appointment to speak with someone tomorrow," I informed Bree.

"Yeah, I heard … so did everyone else here."

I picked up one of the tacos and bit into it. "Oh that's good."

Lisa returned to our table. "How is everything?"

"Fantastic," I said.

"Really good," said Bree.

"Can I get you another margarita?"

"Yes, please."

When Lisa walked away, I said, "Hey, remind me to

swing by Walgreen's on our way home."

"What do you need there?" Bree asked.

"I wanted to grab a couple bags of those miniature Reese's Peanut Butter Cups."

"What for?"

"Just to keep on my desk at work."

Chapter Nine

It was around nine-thirty the following morning when Lint hung up his phone and spun his chair around toward me; I was sitting at my desk.

"Okay, get this," Lint said. "I just got off the phone with Tru-Time. Seems the Carmichaels and the Truitts all started the race within seconds of each other. Roger Truitt crossed the finish line at"—he glanced down at his notes—"9:48:06, and Bambi Carmichael crossed at 9:54:29."

I waited for more information and then asked, "What about Marnie and Brock?"

Lint smiled. "They never crossed the finish line."

"That's strange. What are the odds of a chip malfunction?"

"I asked that same question. The guy I talked to said it happens now and then."

"But to two people in the same race that know each other?"

"He said the chances of that are pretty slim."

"You have a map of the route?"

"Yeah, I'll print it out."

My phone rang. "Jake Stellar," I answered. "You don't say ... When? How long? Can you email me all the information? Okay, thanks." I hung up.

Lint slid the race route onto my desk. "Who was that?"

"Wilmington PD. They fished a thirty-eight-year-old male out of The Cape Fear River last Wednesday. The guy—Conner Lindell—was shot twice in the chest. They dug the slugs out and ballistics matched them to the same weapon that killed Roger Truitt."

"When are they placing time of death?" Lint asked.

"They said the body was in the water at least three days and in pretty bad shape. Coroner says the time of death could be anywhere from Friday evening to Sunday morning. They're sending us everything they have."

"I wonder where our friend Brock Carmichael was from that Friday till Sunday?"

"We'll be sure and ask." I looked up at the clock. "He should be here any minute."

No sooner did I get the words out of my mouth, the phone on my desk rang; Brock Carmichael was at the front desk to see me. "Send him on back," I said.

Brock didn't appear to be in a very good mood when he entered the room. I guess he's not a morning person. He was still clipping his guest badge to the front of his shirt when he entered the squad room. "This better be important, Stellar," he said, not looking up from the badge. Getting the badge to hang perfectly straight seemed to be far too vital to him.

"It's important to me, or I wouldn't have asked you here." I stood and motioned toward the lounge. I went in first, followed by Brock, who shut the door behind him.

"Take a load off," I said hospitably.

Brock chose the leather sofa and put his feet up on the coffee table. I sat in one of the two chairs opposite him.

"Can I get you anything to drink?" I asked. "Coffee, soda?"

"No," Brock answered. "I'm fine. Let's just get this over with." He fussed with the guest badge some more.

The door opened and Lint stuck his head in the room. "Jake, that email came in."

"Thanks, Avis. Can you print everything, put it in a folder, and bring it in?"

"Roger that," Lint answered, and closed the door.

I stood. "Can you excuse me for a second? A cup of coffee sounds really good right now. Do you mind?"

"Not at all."

"You sure you don't want one? There's donuts, too." I tried to calculate how old those Krispy Kremes were by now. Probably eligible for Medicare.

"I'm good."

I left the room and pulled the door shut. The blinds between the lounge and squad room were open and Brock was watching as I made my coffee. He seemed a little nervous, even a bit fidgety, but not as nervous as you would expect someone to be who had just murdered a friend.

I returned to the room with my cup and sat it on the coffee table.

Lint walked into the room, sat in the chair next to me,

and handed me the folder. I opened it and scanned the first page; it was a print out from Tru-Time showing that Brock and Marnie had not crossed the finish line. The second page was a map of the race course.

"What was that race you ran Sunday morning?" I asked. "A 10k?"

"Yes."

"You look pretty fit. What do you run, a seven, eight-minute mile?"

"Little less than nine," Brock answered.

"How did you do Sunday?"

"I did just fine. What does this have to do with anything?"

I pulled the top print out from the folder and laid it on the table in front of him. He removed his feet from the coffee table, sat up, and leaned in closer.

"Because according to this report here, you never crossed the finish line."

"Yes, I did."

"Not according to the chip in your racing bib."

"Maybe the chip malfunctioned."

"We thought of that, but oddly enough, Marnie Truitt never crossed the finish line either."

"I guess they should hire a new company to do the timing next year."

"Yeah, maybe." I placed the race route on the table. "Detective Lint emailed yours and Marnie's photographs to all of the hotels along the race route, and to the cab companies, to see if anyone recognizes you." Now he was almost as nervous as somebody who had just murdered someone.

He feigned confusion. "Why would anyone recognize me?"

"Because here's what we think happened, Brock. We think you and Mrs. Truitt *started* the race, met at one of the hotels along the way, and went in for a little quickie. After you were finished playing doctor, you called a cab and got a ride to the finish line."

"That's a good story, Detective, but that's all it is—a story."

"It's only a matter of time before we hear back from the hotel where you stayed," Lint pointed out. "And the hotel probably has security cameras. Most of the taxi cabs have cameras in them as well."

"The only piece of the puzzle that's missing," I pointed out, "is how did you get from the outlet mall back to the Ocean Bay Club, kill Roger Truitt, and then get back to the mall without the women finding out."

"Maybe Mrs. Truitt was in on it," Lint surmised. "Maybe she kept your wife so busy shopping that she never noticed you had left. Maybe you told her you went off by yourself to shop. Maybe you told her you just went out to the car and waited for them to finish their shopping."

"I didn't kill Roger. And anyway, who's going to believe a far-fetched story like that?" Brock asked. His voice was shaky and his hands trembled, but he tried his best to look calm.

"I'm hoping twelve people are going to believe it," I answered. Then I pulled out the photograph of Conner Lindell, one that was taken before he went into the Cape Fear River. "Do you recognize this man?"

"Should I?" Brock asked.

I pulled out one of the post mortem photos and laid it

next to the first one. "This is what he looks like now."

Brock pulled back and winced. "Jesus Christ, Stellar! Why are you showing me these?"

"That's Conner Lindell, he was pulled out of the Cape Fear River last week. Forensics removed two slugs from his chest that match the one taken from the Truitts' ceiling."

"Was Mr. Lindell a friend of yours, also?" Lint asked.

"I've never seen that man in my life." Carmichael stood. "If you had anything solid you would have arrested me by now. Am I free to leave?"

"For now," I replied. "But we'll be in touch."

Carmichael walked to the door. "You be in touch all you want. You're not pinning this murder on me. I didn't kill anyone."

"We'll also be in touch with your wife when one of the hotel employees recognizes you. I would imagine you'll have a lot of explaining to do."

"You can't do that," said Brock.

"Yes we can," I told him. "And don't try to leave town or we'll have you picked up."

Brock Carmichael stormed out of the room and slammed the door behind him.

"That went well," Lint said.

"It would have been better if he confessed."

Chapter Ten

It took Lint and me a little less than an hour and a half to drive into Wilmington, North Carolina. As we drove slowly along Montrose Lane, Lint stared out the passenger side window at the posh homes, each more spectacular than the last. It was like being in an old episode of *Lifestyles of the Rich and Famous*. If that annoying Robin Leach turned up, I'd have to run him over … with pleasure.

Lint gave an awed whistle. "My God! How much money do you have to make in a year to afford a shack like these?"

"I'm guessing none of them belong to detectives," I responded.

"Here it is," Lint said, as he pointed toward a three-story brick and stone mansion.

I swung into the horse shoe driveway and noticed Lint's jaw was hanging open exactly the same as it was when he saw Marnie Truitt in her yoga pants. "Close your mouth," I said.

I shut off the engine and we climbed from the car—me with ease; Lint, not so much. "You could literally set two of my houses in their garage," Lint said. It was the first time I had ever heard him use the word "literally" correctly.

We walked past a pearl-colored BMW 7 Series and up to the double doors. Lint was carrying a file folder. I grabbed hold of one of the huge rings that hung below one of the two giant brass lion's heads that were mounted on each door.

"This lady's got huge knockers," said Lint.

"Shh!" I replied, and reached for my badge. I was grinning because I had thought the same thing about the knockers. Who wouldn't?

The door opened. A tall, thin, Hispanic woman in a black and white maid's uniform stood before us; she was a head taller than both of us. Her dark hair was pulled up into a severe bun that perched on top of her head, looking like an animal that might bite. She said nothing.

"Detectives Stellar and Lint," I said, showing my badge.

She pulled the door open the rest of the way and said, "Please, come in. Mrs. Lindell is expecting you." I expected her to have an accent, but she didn't. Her deadpan voice was the perfect complement to her bland face.

We walked into a foyer the size of my living room, dining room, and kitchen put together. There were double doors to the right and left of us. In front of us was a hallway between two staircases. The staircase to the right went to the second floor, and the one on the left wound around and over top of the other and led to the third floor. I wondered how one would get from the second floor to the third floor, and figured there must be another staircase somewhere in the house.

"Please wait here," the giantess said. She walked down the hallway in front of us. She didn't hunch like a lot of women her height but carried herself with imperial grace. I got the impression she ran the household, or at least thought she did. I watched her until she disappeared through a doorway on the left.

"How much you think a house like this goes for?" Lint whispered. "Or that Beamer, for that matter."

"I don't know, and please don't ask."

"I'm not going to ask. I'm not *that* stupid."

I never knew what to expect with Lint. I had never pin pointed exactly *how* stupid he was. "Says you," I shot back.

The double doors to the left opened and the giantess appeared as if by magic. *That was some trick*, I thought.

"She will see you now," said the woman.

"You look exactly like the tall drink of water who answered the door," Lint joked, as we walked by her. She didn't think it was funny.

We walked into a study; everything was dark and wooden, except for the furniture, which was dark and leather. Almost every wall was lined with book-filled shelves. The doors silently closed behind us.

A blond woman in her mid-forties, by my estimation, sat behind a desk. She was darkly tanned, and the freckles across the bridge of her nose made her look much younger than her age. Her lips were full, almost too full. I was sure they were stuffed with something, just as I was sure her large breasts were stuffed with something, as well. Maybe thousand dollar bills.

"Please, have a seat," she said, motioning toward the two chairs facing the desk. Lint sat in one and I took the other. Lint handed me the folder.

I was sure she already knew who we were, but I said, "I'm Detective Jake Stellar and this is Detective Avis Lint."

"It's nice to meet you both," she said. "I'm Paralee Lindell."

"Mrs. Lindell, we just ha—"

"Please, call me Parry. All my friends do."

I doubted we were friends. She probably wouldn't spit on me if I was on fire, but I called her Parry anyway. "Parry, we were wondering if you knew either of these two men," I asked, as I pulled 8x10s of Roger Truitt and Brock Carmichael from the folder and laid them on the desk.

She rolled the chair closer to the desk and leaned forward. "No. Why do you ask?"

"The photograph on the left is a man by the name of Roger Truitt. He was found murdered in his condo Sunday morning. The same gun that killed him was also used to kill your husband."

She looked back down at the photographs; her eyes went from one to the other and then back. "No. I've never seen either of them." Her head turned toward the window and she stared out over the pool. "Is there anything else? I have a spin class in a half hour. I don't want to miss it. It's been a rough couple of weeks and my spinning helps with the stress." Her voice was wistful, faraway.

I wished I had more questions for her, but I didn't. The Wilmington detectives assigned to the case had already beaten me to everything I would have asked. I had really hoped she would recognize one of the men in the photos, and maybe she did. But why would she lie? Why would she not want to help us find her husband's killer? Was she involved?

According to the Wilmington police report, the

Lindell's got along great. They never fought or argued. There was no history of domestic abuse. No history of infidelity. The cops had never been called to the house. They were the perfect couple … just like the Truitts, except another man was rubbing Marnie Truitt's shoulders when the doors were closed. I wondered if someone would be rubbing Parry's shoulders after we left.

The maid was waiting with the door open as we walked down the hall. She followed us through the door and closed it behind her. "Detectives," she said.

We turned back.

She stared silently at us for a second.

"What is it?" I asked.

"Have a nice day, gentlemen," she said hesitantly.

"Thank you," we both answered.

As we got to the car, Lint said, "Well, that was a wasted trip."

"Maybe … maybe not," I replied.

Chapter Eleven

Wednesday was Bree's day off, so I got to sleep till five-thirty instead of five. I laid in bed awake listening to her make coffee and play with the dog in the kitchen. The sound of that dogs toenails on the ceramic tile was annoying as shit and I knew I wasn't going to fall back asleep.

I yanked back the covers, threw my legs over the edge of the bed, and slipped into my boxers. I always slept in the buff because it was comfortable. Plus, I figured if any burglars saw me naked, they'd flee in horror.

"Did I wake you?" Bree asked when I walked into the kitchen.

"No, it was that goddamn dog's toenails."

"I'll have to take her to get them trimmed."

"I was dreaming that Sammy Davis Jr. and Gregory Hines came over for breakfast."

"What would make you dream about them?"

I gave her a look. "Because the dogs nails sounded like—never mind." I grabbed a mug out of the cupboard and poured myself some coffee. I sipped it. "What flavor is this?"

"It's not flavored."

"I miss the Keurig." I walked out into the garage and hit the overhead door button. The door raised and I proceeded out into the driveway to grab the morning paper. It was still dark as I stood at the curb looking up Twenty-Fifth Avenue toward North Kings Highway and then back down toward Ocean Boulevard. I tucked the paper into my armpit and went back inside.

"Did you want to run with me this morning?" Bree asked.

I sat down at the table. "When are you going?"

"Six-thirty okay?"

I didn't have to be to work till nine, so I said, "Sure."

"I'll make breakfast when we get back."

I unfolded the paper. "Pancakes?"

"I was going to make eggs. Would you rather have pancakes?"

"Yes." I read the headline. OHIO MAN'S MURDER LINKED TO WILMINGTON HOMICIDE.

"I'll make pancakes," Bree said as she walked down the hall toward the bedroom.

I read the story; they got most of it right. I turned to the funnies. I figured there probably hadn't been a murder in Camp Swampy or Id in quite some time.

It takes Bree about twenty-five minutes to get ready for a run. When she's finally ready she looks like a fitness model, dressed as a runner, going to a photo shoot. I don't even bother *starting* to get ready until Bree announces that she *is* ready, which means it'll be about ten more minutes.

The sun was just peeking over the rows of condos and hotels on Ocean Boulevard. We could feel it's warmth on our faces as we stood in the driveway stretching. I had on shorts and a short-sleeved shirt. Bree was wearing yoga pants, a short sleeved shirt, and a light running jacket.

"Ready?" she asked.

"Ready when you are."

Bree turned left out of the driveway, headed up Twenty-Fifth Avenue and took a right onto Madison Drive. We were running side by side, something I would continue to do on these runs, as long as I kept my weight down, which for some reason seemed a little more difficult lately. Maybe it was the *Krispy Kreme Kurse*.

As we ran behind the Plantation Pancake House I said, "Should we just stop for breakfast?"

"Nope," Bree answered.

"Just joking," I said. I wasn't really joking. I would have stopped in a heartbeat.

Bree turned right onto Twentieth. We ran down Twentieth to Ocean Boulevard and took a left.

We ran past the Hampton Inn and then the Castaway Beach Inn. I thought about Marnie Truitt and Brock Carmichael. The 10k they ran would have taken them right down Ocean Boulevard. They could have stopped at any one of these places. I wondered which one … I wondered if I was even right and they had stopped somewhere at all. Carmichael did seem a little nervous that his wife might find something out, but he didn't seem to be too worried about being accused of murder.

Another half a block and we were in front of Molly Darcy's Irish Pub and my mind went from murder to whiskey wings. "We should eat here tonight," I suggested.

"Sounds good to me," she agreed.

We turned down the Sixteenth Avenue beach access path and slowed to a walk when we reached the sand.

I walked about halfway to the water and kicked off my sneakers. I reached down and pulled off my socks. "Ahh, that feels good," I said, wiggling my toes in the warm sand.

Bree took off her shoes as well. "I'll give Aida a call later," she said.

I walked ankle deep into the water. "For what?"

"See if her and Luca want to have dinner with us tonight."

Ugh. Luca Trentinni. Part-time body builder. Part-time ninja. Full time banker and pain in the ass. Just the sound of his name was like fingernails across a chalkboard. "Good God, no!" I exclaimed.

"Why?"

"*Why?* You know why. I can't stand him."

"I don't understand what's so bad about him."

I turned and held up my fingers one at a time as I recited the list. "He does karate, or some shit, which he feels the need to talk about continuously. He goes to the gym every day; another topic he has to yap about all the time. And he works at a bank and makes four times what I make."

We held hands as we continued to walk along the beach and Bree said, "So you don't like him because he makes more money than you?"

"That's the only part you heard? What about the gym and the karate? It's like the trifecta of bull shit, for chrissakes."

"I've heard him offer to take you with him to karate

class and the gym."

"Yeah, but if I took karate and went to the gym, I would hate myself as much as I hate him."

"You're just being ridiculous. I'll call Bertie then and see if her and Avis would like to come with us."

"Good God!"

"What now?"

"I don't want to spend the evening with Lint either."

"You know, it makes it a little difficult to do anything because you hate everybody."

"I don't hate everybody, just the people we know."

"Take your pick: It's Aida and Luca or Avis and Bertie."

"Tough choice."

"Not for normal people."

"Let me think. Avis or Luca, Luca or Avis. It's like choosing which foot I would like to be kicked in the balls with."

"That's coming next."

"Ouch. I guess you can call Bertie."

Bree yanked me closer to her and planted a kiss on my cheek. "You'll have fun, you'll see."

"It's like you just met me."

Chapter Twelve

When we got back to the house, I took a quick shower and made it to the station by 8:45. This time I remembered to bring the huge bag of Reese's Peanut Butter Cups I had bought two nights before. I found a glass bowl in the cabinet under the coffee maker, filled it full of the candy, and sat it on the corner of my desk. *Perfect*, I thought. *Let's see if Lint can pass that up*. I grabbed one of the Reese's and ate it. *Wow, those are good*.

I took a seat at my desk and Lint walked in. "Mornin', Jake," he said.

"Mornin', Lint."

I pretended to be looking at paperwork on my desk while stealing glances at Lint. He looked at the candy, but didn't say a word. When he got to his desk he stowed his weapon in his top left drawer. "Anything back from those hotels?" he asked.

"Nothing yet," I answered. I grabbed another candy, unwrapped it, and ate it. As I chewed I let out a little "*Mmm-mmm*."

Lint glanced over. "What do you have there?"

"Just some peanut butter cups. Help yourself."

He held up his hand. "No, better not."

Dammit!

The phone at Lint's desk rang and he picked it up. "Detective Lint speaking." He listened for a few seconds and then said, "They did, did they? ... No, that's okay, we'll stop over in a bit and pick it up. Thank you."

"One of the hotels?" I asked.

"You got it," Lint answered.

"Which one?"

"The Castaway, on Ocean Boulevard."

"I knew it. Bree and I passed it on our morning run. A likely place for an illicit rendezvous."

Lint pulled his gun out of the drawer and shoved it in the holster clipped to his belt. "Shall we head over?"

"Yeah. What do they have for us?"

"The kid who worked the desk Sunday recognized Marnie and Brock from the photographs we left. They said they have Brock on camera paying for the room."

I grabbed my weapon and we headed over to the Castaway Beach Inn. Just for shits and giggles I also brought along photographs of Conner and Parry Lindell. Who knows, maybe the same guy would recognize them as well. It was worth a shot.

"When are you going to let me drive this thing?" Lint asked as he climbed from the car.

"Maybe never," I replied.

The Castaway Beach Inn was a light brown stucco building that stood three stories tall. There were around twenty-seven rooms with each room exiting the front of the building onto a walkway that was open to the street. The office, a separate building, was only one story and sat close to the road with its parking lot to the right. The rooms sat behind the parking lot, closer to the beach.

Lint pulled open the front door to the office, and I walked in first while reaching for my shield.

"Good morning gentlemen," said the woman behind the counter. She was a short woman, almost as wide as she was tall. She had long black hair with a lot of gray mixed in. Even though she had almost no wrinkles on her face I guessed her age to be around fifty. Her nametag read WANDA.

"Good morning," I replied. "I'm Detective Jake Stellar, and this is Detective Avis Lint. We got a call from the manager this morning about the photos one of our officers left."

"Yes," she answered. "Let me run out back and get him for you."

I put away my badge. "Thank you."

Wanda came around the desk and went out the front door. "I'll be right back."

I turned around to see Lint standing in front of a floor rack full of fliers and maps to local tourist traps. "You ever been to Alligator Adventure?" he asked.

"Years ago," I replied.

He pulled out the flier, folded it, and shoved it in his front pocket. "I've never been. I wonder if Bertie has."

The woman returned and said, "He'll be right in. Some college kids completely trashed one of the rooms last night. Kids today, they have no respect for other people's property."

The manager walked in shortly after and introduced

himself as Ron Briggs. He asked Wanda to step out from behind the counter for a minute so he could operate the computer. He punched a few keys and then turned the monitor around so Lint and I could see it.

"This first footage is from when the gentleman *paid* for the room," Briggs said.

I looked at the monitor and then quickly glanced behind him to locate the camera; it was mounted to the ceiling and angled in a way to catch the front door and the desk. We watched Brock Carmichael walk into the office, approach the desk, and pay for the room in cash.

"What time is that?" I asked.

"1:32 p.m.," Briggs replied, referring to the time stamp in the upper right hand corner of the monitor.

Lint moved in closer for a better look. "Can't be," he said. "The race didn't even start on Sunday until nine."

"Oh, this wasn't Sunday," Briggs said. "This was Saturday afternoon. He paid for the room on Saturday, for two nights."

"So they were all checked in and had the key before the race even started," I said.

"Yes," Ron answered.

"That saved them some time," Lint pointed out. "They didn't have to pay for the room Sunday during the race."

"You said the guy on duty recognized the photos we left," I said. "Is he here today?"

"No, he had yesterday and today off. He just stopped in last night to pick up his paycheck. That's when he noticed the photographs the officer had left."

"Can I get his contact information?" I asked.

Briggs pulled open a drawer beneath the computer.

"Sure," he said as he shuffled through a small deck of index cards. "Here it is." He handed one of the cards to me.

Wally Crane, the card read, and below it a cell phone number and address. I handed the card to Lint and he stuck it in his shirt pocket.

I asked Briggs to pull up footage from the exterior hotel complex for Sunday morning.

"Here's the footage from Sunday," Briggs stated.

The video feed was from a camera mounted on the south corner of the rear building; it showed the entire parking lot and the side of the office building. Lint and I watched as several runners ran down Ocean Boulevard. Brock Carmichael and Marnie Truitt entered the frame and took a hard left off of Ocean Boulevard, and they ran together toward their room. As they got to the front of the building they disappeared from the camera's view. The time stamp read 9:06 a.m. Briggs then fast-forwarded to 9:55 a.m., the time they ran out to the street, jumped in a cab, and sped away.

"What room were they in?" Lint asked.

Briggs jabbed at the keyboard. "Room number 108," he said.

"Can you make us a copy of everything you just showed us?" I asked.

"Of course," Briggs replied. He rummaged through the same drawer again and pulled out a thumb drive. "If you can stick around for a few minutes I'll download it onto this."

"Has anyone checked into that room since Carmichael?" I asked.

Briggs returned to the keyboard. "We had a couple Monday night and they checked out Tuesday morning."

"Can you hold off on renting it out again until we have our guys come down and have a look around?"

"I sure can." He inserted the thumb drive, hit a few keys, slid the mouse around the pad, and said. "There, it should just take a few minutes. This thing is pretty old and slow."

"Aren't we all," Lint joked.

Chapter Thirteen

Wally Crane was twenty years old and lived with his parents at 319 Sixty-First Avenue North. I pulled into the driveway, backed out, and parked on the street. The white vinyl-sided house sat on pillars and had a wooden staircase that led to a front porch.

"Detectives Stellar and Lint, ma'am," I announced when a woman apparently in her late fifties answered the door.

"Is something wrong?" she asked.

"No, ma'am. Are you Mrs. Crane?"

"Yes."

"We were wondering if your son, Wally, was at home."

"Yes, he is."

"Can we speak to him please?"

"What is this about?"

Once upon a time she would have just said, "Yes, Detectives, he's here. Come on in and I'll get him for you." But now, thanks to YouTube and Facebook, everyone suddenly knows their rights.

"Ma'am, we would just like to ask him a few questions," I sighed.

"Should I call a lawyer? Do you have a warrant?"

Lint stepped forward. "Listen, lady, your son has information vital to our homicide investigation. Furthermore, he's twenty years old—we don't need your permission to talk to him. Now, we can do this the easy way—you asking us to come in—or we can call for a couple units to come down here with their lights on and their sirens blasting. They can pull up in front of your house for all of your neighbors to see and we can have the officers put young Wally in the back of one of the patrol cars and bring him down to the station to answer some questions. What's it gonna be?"

Mrs. Crane experienced an immediate attitude adjustment. She glanced past us at one of her neighbors who was already watching from a window. "There's no need to be rude. Come in, please."

"Thank you," we both said.

We were shown to the living room where we had a seat on the couch while she went down the hall to retrieve her son.

From the blond bed head and blanket creases on the side of Wally's pale face, it looked as though we had awakened him from his beauty sleep—something the young man could not afford to lose. Oddly enough, Wally Crane looked an awful lot like Ichabod Crane. He was tall, angular, and as skinny as a pipe cleaner; his long neck and prominent Adam's apple suggested a goose that had swallowed a golf ball.

"What's up, man?" Wally asked, his voice rattling with slumber grumble. He loudly cleared his throat and then swallowed whatever he had brought up.

Lint and I looked at each other without expression and then back at Wally.

"Your manager at the hotel said you recognized the man and woman from the photos one of our officers left," I said.

"When did this happen?" Mrs. Crane asked. "Wally, you didn't tell me anything about this."

Wally ignored his mother and took a seat on the arm of a chair directly across from Lint and me. "I recognized *him*, but I didn't see *her*," Wally explained. "I didn't see *her* until Mr. Briggs played back the security tape." He yawned and rubbed both eyes with the palms of his hands.

"So, you never saw Mrs. Truitt."

"Who's Mrs. Truitt?"

"The woman in the photo," Lint replied.

"Oh, no, dude. I never saw her."

"Wally, when did this happen?" his mother asked again. "Why didn't you tell me and your father about this?"

"Mom, stop. God! Go make me some breakfast or something." Mrs. Crane begrudgingly left the room and Wally turned back to us. "Sorry, dudes. The old lady gets a little too protective sometimes."

"No problem, dude," Lint responded.

I held out my hand and Lint handed me the folder he was holding. I opened it on my lap and pulled out photographs of Bambi Carmichael, Roger Truitt, and Conner Lindell. I closed the folder and placed the photos on the coffee table.

"Wally, have you ever seen any of *these* people before?" I asked.

Wally slowly scanned the photographs. "No, none of them. Just the other lady," he said pointing at my lap.

"What other lady?" I asked, looking down.

"The one there in the folder. The other picture I saw when you opened it."

I opened the folder again to reveal the photograph of Parry Lindell.

"Her," said Wally. "I've seen her before."

I took out the picture and laid it on the table with the others. "Where did you see her?" I asked.

"At the hotel. Once about two weeks ago, and another time about a week before that."

I put my finger on the photograph of Conner Lindell. "Was this man with her?"

"No, a younger guy. Maybe thirty, thirty-one, something like that."

"You're positive it was her?" Lint asked.

"One hundred percent, dude. I remember because of her car. It was a light colored Beamer, a real expensive one." Wally thought for a second. "Also her ass, man. For an old lady she had an ass that wouldn't quit, dudes."

"Did she arrive with the guy or did they drive separately?" I asked.

"No, the dude had his own wheels. Nice car too, a Porsche. Not new like hers, probably ten years old or so."

"And you only remember her being at the hotel just the two times?" Lint asked.

"Yeah."

"Wally, you want your eggs scrambled?" Mrs. Crane called out from the kitchen.

"Whatever, Mom. I don't give a shit," Wally called back, and then gave us an eye roll and a head shake as though we both understood the day to day grind of being a worthless douche.

"Thanks, Wally," I said. "If we have any more questions we'll be in touch."

"Whatever you need, dudes," he replied, and then showed us to the door.

On our way back to the car Lint said, "I'm getting hungry, Jake."

"Me too," I agreed. "Where do you want to go?"

Trying his hardest to sound like Wally Crane, Lint answered. "Whatever, dude. I don't give a shit."

Chapter Fourteen

We ate at Friendly's, on North Kings Highway whose service lived up to its name. I should have had Lint order first because after I ordered my bacon cheeseburger and fries, he ordered a goddamn crispy chicken salad with fat free Italian dressing. I was so pissed at his demonstration of willpower that I ordered an orange Fribble, the restaurant's signature shake, to go and made quite a show of slurping it down to the last delectable drop. Lint showed absolutely no interest, which pissed me off even more. Meanwhile, I swear I could feel my belt constricting on me like a boa.

We were back to the station before one-thirty. We hadn't been at our desks for more than a few minutes when my desk phone rang. It was a Detective Grace from the Wilmington PD informing me that Parry Lindell had been found floating face down in her pool this morning.

*****

I pulled the car to the curb in front of the Lindell home; there were two Wilmington patrol cars, a white Crime Scene van, and two unmarked units sitting in the driveway. We walked past the pearl BMW and up to the front door. The door was wide open and an officer was standing just inside the foyer. When he turned I flashed my badge; Lint did the same. Officer Crown led us through the house and out to the pool.

Two detectives stood at the edge of the pool as Crime Scene personnel and other officers moved about the backyard.

"Detective Grace," one of the men said, holding out his hand. "My partner, Detective Lynch."

We introduced ourselves and then I asked, "Who found her?"

"The maid," Lynch answered. He flipped through pages of a note pad he was holding. "Maid's name is Cora Gonzales. She said she got here this morning around eight. She let herself in and started breakfast. At nine-thirty when Mrs. Lindell still hadn't come down, Ms. Gonzales went upstairs to check on her. She wasn't up there and her bed hadn't been slept in."

Detective Grace began where Lynch left off. "She also said it wasn't unusual that Mrs. Lindell didn't sleep here. She has a friend she has stayed with few times since her husband's death, but the car being in the driveway made her a little suspicious, so she walked out here and that's when she found the body in the water."

"What did the ME come up with for a time of death?" I asked.

"He's placing it between eight and eleven last night," Grace replied.

"Cause of death?" Lint asked.

"Blunt force trauma to the back of the head he's guessing. He'll know more when he gets her on the table."

"Murder weapon?" I asked.

"Haven't found anything yet," Lynch answered.

I asked if the maid was still on the property. They told me no, that she had called her husband at work around noon to come and pick her up. They gave us her contact information if we wanted to speak to her.

"You guys have anyone you like for *your* homicide yet?" Grace asked.

"Originally we were thinking it was a guy—Brock Carmichael—who had been staying with the Truitts with his wife. He had the means, and the opportunity, but no motive that we can come up with."

"He *is* jumpin' the dead guy's wife, though" Lint added. "But we can't arrest him for being an asshole."

"We have video of Mrs. Truitt and Carmichael getting a room at a hotel together," I informed them. "We also have an employee of the same hotel who can place Mrs. Lindell there on occasion as well."

"When?" Lynch asked.

"The kid said, a couple weeks ago and once a week or so before that."

"I'm guessing she wasn't there with her husband," said Grace.

"Correct," Lint answered. "It was a guy in his early thirties, drives an older Porsche."

I glanced down at the piece of paper I was holding and read the address for Cora Gonzales. "I think we will go have a talk with Ms. Gonzales," I said. "When we left here the other day it seemed like there was something she wanted to tell us."

We shook hands again and Detective Grace reminded us to keep him informed of anything we might learn from Ms. Gonzales. I said we would.

Just then an officer emerged from the hedges that surrounded the property. "I've got something over here!" he shouted.

The four of us looked over. The officer was holding a golf club by his fingertips, it appeared to be a sand wedge.

Two members of the Crime Scene unit ran over to inspect the club. One of them turned back toward Detective Grace and shook his head yes. The other guy pulled a large clear evidence bag from his back pocket. He unfolded the bag and held it open while the officer dropped it in.

"Looks like we got a weapon now," Lynch said, stating the obvious.

"Now we just have to find the guy who played through here last night," Grace said with a grim chuckle.

Chapter Fifteen

Hector and Cora Gonzales lived in a pretty nice two bedroom home on Fifth Avenue South—nice enough to make me wonder exactly how much a full-time maid earned per year. We knocked on the door, showed our badges, and were invited in.

Cora was in pajamas and a robe when she walked into the living room. When I first saw her haunting the Lindell mansion like an outsized ghost, she had seemed cold, mysterious, and vaguely menacing. Now, in her own home and so casually attired, she struck me as ordinary and almost vulnerable—accent on the almost. His wife was about to take a nap, Hector explained. We said we understood and wouldn't take up too much of their time.

I got right to the point and said, "Cora"—she asked that I call her Cora; her sudden friendliness threw me for a loop—"it seemed like there was something you wanted to tell us as we were leaving the other day."

She gave me a phony look of confusion.

"What do you mean?" she asked.

"If there's something you know, you should tell us," I said softly. I didn't give her the hollow threats of withholding evidence or obstruction of justice, like I would in most situations. "You want to do everything in your power to help us, don't you?"

She looked to her husband, then to Lint and back at me. "I'm sure it's nothing."

"What some people think is nothing can sometimes help fill in a pretty big gap," Lint said.

Wow, Lint, that was a pretty good line, I thought.

Cora looked at Hector once again and he gave her a nod. "I don't know if this has anything to do with what's happened," she said, "but … they belonged to this club."

"Mr. and Mrs. Lindell," I said.

"Yes."

"What kind of a club?" Lint asked.

"They would have these parties at the members' homes." She glanced quickly at Hector and seemed almost too embarrassed to continue. Her face reddened. "They would sleep with each other's wives."

Lint raised an eyebrow. "A swingers club?"

Cora shook her head yes.

Lint and I looked at each other and then back at Cora. "Did they speak openly about this?" I asked.

"No, never. But we just knew."

"We?" I asked.

"Me," Cora said. "And the rest of the staff. Harvey, the gardener, and Chad, the pool guy. The Lindells never spoke of the parties with us, but Chad knew one of the couples who attended them. After a while we just put two and two together."

"Are Chad and Harvey fulltime members of the staff?" Lint asked.

Cora shook her head. "No, they both come once a week. They have their own businesses."

"Do you know if the Wilmington Police Department questioned Chad and Harvey?" I inquired.

"Yes. They questioned both of them."

Lint asked: "Did any of you mention the parties?"

"I didn't. I don't think either one of them did either."

"Do you have any idea how long these parties have been going on or how long the Lindells have been in the club?"

"At least three years," Cora answered. "That's how long I've been working for the Lindells. The way Chad talked, it was the Lindells who started the club."

Lint went to the car to retrieve the folder containing the photographs of the Carmichaels and the Truitts. Cora and her husband looked at the photos but didn't recognize any of them.

We asked Cora if she could make us a list of the other member's names. She said the only couple she knew by name was the couple Chad Harper—the pool boy—knew. Lint handed her the note pad he kept in his back pocket and the pen he kept in his shirt pocket and she jotted down the names Fred and Lucy Wilkes.

After asking a few more questions we thanked Hector and Cora for their time and said we would be in touch if we had any more questions.

On the ride back to North Myrtle Beach, Lint and I ran questions by each other. Among others, were the Carmichaels and Truitts members of the same swingers club as the Lindells and Wilkes? Was this swingers club the connection we had been looking for? Should we notify the Wilmington PD and tell them that Fred and Lucy's lives might be in danger?

*****

"Run a check on Fred and Lucy Wilkes," I told Lint when we got back to our desks. "Then get a hold of Grace and Lynch in Wilmington—let them know about the sex club and the Wilkes."

"I'm on it," he answered, as he stowed his weapon in his desk drawer.

"Cup of coffee?" I asked, heading toward the coffee machine.

"Sure."

I poured us each a mug, sat Lint's on his desk in front of him, and went in to talk with Captain Stein.

Merle was sitting behind his desk and looked up as I walked into his office. His bushy eyebrows rose causing the three deep wrinkles in his darkly tanned forehead to show. He laid his pen down on whatever form he was filling out. "What do you got?" he asked.

"They're all swingers," I announced, closing his door behind me and taking a seat on the leather couch against the wall.

Merle cocked his head and grinned. "Sexy."

"I guess."

He leaned back in his chair and clasped his fingers behind his head. "Let's hear about it."

"According to their maid, the Lindells are in a swingers club that meets about once a month. She didn't have a lot of details but she gave us the name of another couple that belong. Lint is notifying the Wilmington detectives leading the investigation."

"The Truitt's members?" Merle asked.

"Not sure yet. I'm gonna give Marnie Truitt a call and have her stop in this afternoon."

"Sounds good."

"Also, a kid who works at the hotel where Marnie and Brock Carmichael stayed the morning of the race recognized Parry Lindell from a photo. Said she stayed there a few times with a younger man who drives a Porsche."

"We know who this guy is?"

"No, the kid says he parked his car in the beach access parking lot; the security camera didn't get a shot of the license plate."

Merle ran his fingernails through his slicked back, jet-black hair. "So they have the hotel and the club in common."

"We're thinking."

"Truitt know you got her on camera at the hotel?"

"Not yet." I got up from the couch and walked toward the door.

Merle said, "Hey."

I tuned back. "Yeah?"

"How's Lint doing?"

"Good. Why?"

"Just keep an eye on him for the next few days. Getting shot has ruined better cops than him."

"He's fine," I assured Merle, and left the office.

When I returned to my desk Lint was on his phone.

"Sounds great," Lint said. "I love you, too." He hung up the phone and turned to me with a smile I had only seen on his face from behind a *Super*SONIC Bacon Cheeseburger.

"What?" I asked.

"You didn't tell me we were all going out to dinner together tonight."

"Oh yeah, I forgot." *Shit! I had forgot.* I reached into the candy dish, unwrapped a peanut butter cup, and tossed it into my mouth. "Want one?" I asked.

Lint tapped his gut. "Better not."

What the hell? I picked up my phone and called Marnie Truitt.

"Hello?" said Marnie.

"Mrs. Truitt, it's Detective Stellar."

"Oh, Jake. How can I help you?"

"I was wondering if you could come over to the station and answer a few questions."

There was a moment of silence and then she said, "It would be better for me if I could come tomorrow morning."

"It would be better for *everyone* if you came now," I informed her.

"So, you're not asking me, you're telling me."

"That's right."

"You don't have the right to tell me—"

"Marnie, I have the right to tell Bambi Carmichael that we have video of you and Brock arriving at the Castaway Beach Inn Sunday morning shortly after the start of the race. Be here by four and we'll keep that just between us … for now." I hung up the phone.

Chapter Sixteen

Brock Carmichael gave Marnie Truitt a ride to the station. When she arrived she had no complaints, probably because she wanted me to keep our little secret. Rather than question her in the lounge, I had Lint take her into the interrogation room. I let her sit in there by herself for about fifteen minutes before I entered. Before she arrived I had placed a blank piece of paper and a pen on the table in front of the chair she was now sitting in. I made Brock wait at my desk.

"Thanks for coming down," I said, and closed the door behind me. I tossed a file folder on the table.

"Did I have a choice?" Marnie asked.

"We all have choices, Mrs. Truitt. Some just choose the wrong ones." I pulled out the chair across from her and took a seat. I removed the photographs of Conner Parry Lindell and placed them on the table next to the sheet of paper.

"Who are *they*?" she asked. It was not convincing.

"What's the matter, Mrs. Truitt, don't you recognize them with their clothes on? This is Conner and Parry Lindell, I believe they belong to the same club as you."

"Club?"

"Let's cut the shit, Marnie. Okay? We know all about the sex club." Her face turned a shade of crimson I don't think I had ever seen in my life. "Now, what I need you to do is write down the names of everyone in the club."

"I don't know everyone in the club," she protested.

"Do your best." She began writing. "We already know Fred and Lucy Wilkes," I informed her.

When she was done writing she laid the pen down on the table and slid the list over to me. She leaned back in her chair, folded her arms in front of her, and turned her head toward the wall. She looked like a high school girl who had just ratted out her friends.

There were four couples listed, including the Wilkes.

"That's it?" I asked. "Not a very large club."

"There's more, I think, but we're only here for a few months out of the year. Every member doesn't come to every meeting, and no one discusses the members who aren't in attendance."

I read the names aloud. "Mike and Cathy Paine, Phil and Sue Fitz, Fred and Lucy Wilkes, and Nora and Lee Parks." I laid the paper down. "All married couples?"

Marnie nodded. "Yes. That's one of the rules."

"Rules? Huh, just like Fight Club." I snickered a little; Marnie did not. "So, how many of these rules are there?"

Marnie looked to the ceiling in thought for a second. "Three, I think."

One less than Fight Club, I mused. "And what are they?"

"Only couples. They don't want some weird guy showing up alone just to watch and have sex with other men's wives."

"Makes sense," I remarked. "We wouldn't want anyone weird joining a sex club."

Marnie glared at me. "Should I continue, or do you have more jokes to make?"

"I'm sure I'll have more, but continue."

"The second rule is no sex with other members outside of club meetings."

"A tough one to follow, I'm learning."

"And number three is, deny everything."

"So, you do not talk about Fight Club—I mean, Sex Club."

"Right."

"Not talking about it is what got Parry Lindell killed. Wilmington PD would have protected her if they had known about the club."

"Does that mean you're going to protect me?"

"We'll assign a unit to be with you at all times until we feel there's no longer a threat."

"Thank you," she said quietly.

"You didn't write down the Carmichaels as being members. Why?"

"They're not members. They were guests of my husband and me."

"How many meetings have they been to?"

"Just the one … about four weeks ago."

"How often do these meetings take place?"

"About once every two months or so. Sometimes *once* a month. We go to maybe two while we're here."

"Were the meetings always at the Lindells' home?"

"Most of the time. They have enough bedrooms to accommodate everyone."

"That's handy." I returned the photographs to the file folder and added the list Marnie had given me. "Thank you for your time, Mrs. Truitt. I'll have an officer show you out."

"You're not going to tell Bambi about Brock and me?" Marnie asked as I held the door for her.

"Not for now," I said.

Chapter Seventeen

When I pulled Bree's car to the curb in front of 705 Thirteenth Avenue I was still bitching about having to stop for gas. I put the Volkswagen in park and sniffed my hands.

"My hands are going to smell like gasoline all night now," I complained.

"Bitch, bitch, bitch," was Bree's answer. "I told you I could pump the gas."

I shook my head as I climbed from the car. "And for the one millionth time, I'm not gonna sit in the car while you pump the gas. Why can't you just get gas on your way home?"

"I didn't have time."

That was always her excuse and it didn't make any more sense this time than it did the last billion times I had to stop for gas on the way to a restaurant.

"Just forget it," I said.

"I'm trying," Bree answered.

We walked up the sidewalk to Bertie Clodfelter's house.

"Beautiful house," Bree commented.

"Yup," I replied. "I can't believe I'm doing this."

"Doing what?"

"Going to dinner with Avis Lint. You owe me big time for this."

"Sex, I'm guessing."

"Good guess. And not regular old bed sex either." I knocked on the door. "This is gonna be kitchen table sex, or swimming pool sex."

"Maybe couch se—"

Lint yanked open the door. "Did I hear something about pool sex?" he asked.

Bree's face reddened. "That was just Jake adding something to his wish list." Bree hugged Avis. "How are you feeling, Avis?"

Lint rotated his shoulder and winced. "Good. Still a little sore."

I rolled my eyes and walked on in past him. "Maybe you better switch to the super absorbent pads," I recommended.

"You look like you've lost weight, Avis," Bree pointed out.

Lint slapped his belly. "A few pounds."

I walked down the hall and into the kitchen. Bertie was standing at the counter, looking into a mirror that was attached to the back of one of the cupboard doors. She was inserting a diamond stud into her ear.

"Who's having sex in the pool?" Bertie asked.

"Probably nobody," I answered. I took a seat at the bar.

Lint entered the kitchen behind me and pointed at a crystal bowl at the end of the bar. "I filled up the candy dish with some of those peanut butter cups you love so much," he informed me. "Help yourself."

I grabbed one, unwrapped it, and tossed it into my mouth. "Want one?" I asked, sliding the dish in front of Lint.

"No thanks," he replied. "Don't want to ruin my dinner."

"Now that's will power, Avis," Bree said. "Jake could learn a little of that from you."

"Yeah," I said.

Lint shook his head in agreement. "You're tellin' me. He's ate almost a whole bag at work in the last two days. Keeps trying to get me to eat 'em."

Bree shot me a look. *Crap. Was she on to me?*

"He does, does he?" Bree asked.

Bertie put her arms around Lint and rubbed his belly. "I don't know what I'll do if my big teddy bear loses this belly."

Lint grinned. "She calls me her big teddy bear."

"Yeah, I got that," I sighed.

Bertie suddenly gave a little squeal' "Avis! Are you wearing your gun?" she said, patting his hip.

"Sure. I'm always packin'. So's Jake."

Bertie's jaw dropped. "But we're going on a double date!"

"A cop's on duty 24/7," I said automatically. Bree rolled her eyes at the cliché; I didn't blame her. "So, are we going to go eat, or what?"

The four of us climbed in the car. I made a right hand turn onto Edge Drive and headed south.

"Molly Darcy's?" I asked.

"I made us a reservation at Thoroughbreds," Bertie answered.

Thoroughbreds Chop House and Seafood Grille was great but pricey, on a cop's salary. I gave Bree the old this-is-gonna-cost-me look. She pretended not to notice. I glanced in the rear view mirror, Lint and Bertie were lip-locked. It was like my mirror was tuned into the National Geographic Channel: *When Cougars Attack Fat Men*. Should I bang garbage can lids together or should I spray them with a garden hose? I didn't know; no one had made out in the back seat of my car on a double date in at least thirty years.

We hadn't made it three blocks when Bree pointed up ahead. "Jake, I think that girl's van is broken down."

"Uh-huh," I replied as I drove on by.

"You should stop," she said.

"I'm not a mechanic."

Bree looked to the back seat for an ally.

Lint tapped me on the shoulder. "It's getting dark, Jake, maybe we should go back."

"Yeah, turn around, Jake," said Bertie.

Great, now I'm the bad guy. I pulled to the side of the road and whipped a U-turn.

The young blond with dreadlocks appeared to be about eighteen or nineteen years old. Her old white Chevy conversion van was parked at the edge of the street. From the looks of the vehicle she was lucky it had gotten her this far.

She was dressed in a red tank top that showed her belly ring, white denim cutoffs, and a pair of old leather flip-flops. As we pulled up and parked across the street from her—facing the opposite direction—she pushed herself away from the van and smiled nervously.

I lowered my window. "Everything okay?" I shouted.

Before she had a chance to answer, Sir Eats-a-lot, defender of the weak and downtrodden, was already climbing out of the back seat to assist.

I went ahead and shut off the engine. "Wait in the car," I said to the ladies, and followed Lint to the van.

"She giving you some trouble?" Lint asked.

The girl looked around and then back at us. "No, everything is fine," she said.

Lint chuckled. "Fine? Do you need us to call someone for you?"

"No, I called my boyfriend. He's on his way. Thanks. You can go."

"Pop the hood, we'll take a look," I said.

"That's okay, you don't have to." She glanced back at the house behind her. She seemed to be growing more nervous.

"It's okay, honey," Lint assured her. "We're cops. I'm Avis Lint and this is Jake Stellar" Lint turned back toward the car. "Our wives are right there in the car."

"You're cops?" she asked.

I shook my head yes. This seemed to agitate her even more.

She glanced back at the house behind her once again.

"Please, everything is fine. Can you just go … please?"

I glanced over to where she kept looking and asked, "Are you okay?"

"Yes, everything is fine," she replied. "I'm just waiting for my boyfriend."

"Is someone in that house?" Lint asked quietly.

"What house?"

"The house you keep looking back at," I answered.

Just then the front door of the house opened and two men walked out—the first man with his back to us—carrying a humongous flat screen TV.

Lint went for his weapon. "Hold it!" he shouted. "Police!"

The thieves dropped the television and stumbled over each other, and the TV, to get back inside the house.

Mesmerized by Lint's bravado, I didn't notice the young woman reach into her van window. Big mistake! I was just about to pull my 9mm when the girl spun back around holding a .38 snub-nose revolver inches from my face.

"Don't!" she screamed. Her hands were shaking.

I released the grip on my weapon.

"Put up your hands," she said, because she must have heard someone in a movie say it once.

I slowly raised my hands and when they were level with her .38, I slapped the pistol from her hand. Before it hit the ground I had the front of her shirt in my left fist and was drawing my gun with my right. I spun her around and shoved her up against the van.

"Do you have any weapons on you?" I asked in the angriest voice I had.

"No," she sobbed.

"What's your name?"

"Allison."

I looked back at the car, Bree was already on the phone.

"How many of them are there in there?"

"T-two."

"Do they have weapons?"

"Billy has a pistol."

"How old are they?"

"Billy is nineteen and Buzz is twenty, I think."

"Are the homeowners in there?"

She shook her head no.

"Lint, one of them is armed!" I yelled.

Lint hunkered down behind a palmetto in the front yard—as if the tree's skinny trunk offered any real protection for his bulk. "Come on out!" he hollered. "There's no place for you to go."

No place but the back door, I thought. I forced the young girl to the ground behind the rear tire of the van. "You sit right there and don't move. If you try to run, I swear to God I'll shoot you. You understand?"

She nodded yes. Tears were streaming down her cheeks. I hated to be so harsh with the kid, but she had just stuck a gun in my face.

I bent down, picked up her .38, and shoved it into my front pocket. I took off running around the house to find a clear view of the rear entrance. I heard Lint yell for them to come out again, and few seconds later I heard the sound of sirens. Then I felt the vibration of my cell phone in my pocket.

"Hello?" I answered. It was Lint.

"Hey, pal," he said. "What's the plan?"

"Get back to the van and give your cell phone to the girl. Have her call her boyfriend and tell him to come to the front door. When he opens the door you give me a holler. I'll bust in the back and you go in the front."

"You got it," Lint said, and hung up.

I stood with my back against a huge ash leaf maple tree, my gun drawn and held against my chest. I was about ten feet from the back door.

"Now!" I heard Lint scream, and I took off running.

On my seventh or eighth stride I threw my shoulder into the door, splintering it from its hinges. I hit on my side and rolled to my knees in front of the oven. I peeked around the corner. I could see through the dining room and living room to the front door. One of the men was through the door and running across the yard. Lint tackled him near the front of the van just as a patrol car pulled up.

"Billy!" I shouted. There was no answer. I hollered his name again. "Billy! Throw down your weapon. Allison doesn't want to see you die today."

"Screw you, man! You come in here and get me!" Billy shouted back from somewhere out of sight.

"If I come and get you only one of us is walking out of this house … and you're going out in a body bag."

"It wasn't my idea, man. Buzz said we would be in and out."

"Then slide your weapon across the floor where I can see it."

Another unit pulled up out front and stopped. The

officer in the first car had his gun drawn and was aiming at the front door, over the hood of his car.

"I'm coming out!" Billy shouted. "I give up."

"Throw down your gun—"

It was too late. Billy ran toward the door, his pistol in his hand.

The officer fired twice, hitting Billy once in the thigh and once in the hip.

"Hold your fire! Hold your fire!" I screamed.

Billy lay in the foyer, his gun on the floor. I kicked the weapon into the living room and knelt down next to the boy. Billy looked more like fifteen than nineteen.

"Get a stretcher in here!" I shouted.

"Don't let me die," Billy cried.

"You're gonna be fine," I said. I looked up, Lint was standing over me.

"I wasn't gonna hurt anybody," Billy said. "Allison?"

"Your girlfriend's fine." I glanced at the house. Buzz was standing on the threshold with his hands clasped behind his head while an officer frisked him. "Your accomplice is on the front porch shitting his pants."

"That pussy," Billy wheezed.

Two paramedics wheeled a gurney up to the front door and lifted Billy onto it.

I put my 9mm away as I walked down the sidewalk toward Bree, who was waiting by our car. She smiled and I smiled back.

By this time Allison and Buzz were cuffed and sitting in the backseat of a cruiser.

Bertie was climbing out of the backseat as Lint and I

got to the car. She threw her arms around him, and Bree did the same to me.

"A cop is on duty 24/7," she cooed. "My hero!"

"I guess we missed our reservations," I said. "We better just head over to Molly Darcy's for a quick bite."

"Nonsense!" Bertie exclaimed. "The manager at Thoroughbreds is a good friend of mine, he'll seat us no matter what time we get there."

"Terrific," I said.

Chapter Eighteen

"See, last night wasn't so bad," Bree said, as she stood in front of the stove flipping each strip of bacon one at a time.

I looked up from the funnies. "No, that was awesome," I agreed.

She shot me a look. "I mean dinner with Avis and Bertie."

"Oh, that. I thought you meant the sex."

Bree shook her head. "We'll have to do it again some time."

"How about tonig—"

"Dinner!"

"Oh. Yeah, whatever. Maybe next time we won't stumble upon a robbery in progress. You have any idea how much paperwork I have to do today, just because we went to dinner with them? If I had been sitting in my own living room in front of the television where I belong, that wouldn't have happened." I returned to my reading.

"You saved some old couple from having everything they own stolen from them."

"They probably have insurance."

"Wow. Scrambled, or over medium?"

"Scrambled is fine."

"Bertie mentioned going up to her camp in a few weeks."

"Did she?"

"They get along really good. Her and Avis, I mean."

"It's new. Give it a few years."

"She told me she's going to ask him to move in with her."

"Oh yeah? I bet that will end well."

"You're such a pessimist. Why can't you just be happy for them?"

"I'm ecstatic."

"You sound it."

"You know, I was thinking, if Bertie and Avis were celebrities, the tabloids would refer to them as Beavis. Bertie, Avis ... Beavis. You get it?"

"How long did it take you to come up with that little gem?"

"Three days."

*****

I walked into the station at exactly nine o'clock. Lint was already at his desk, talking on his phone.

"How was dinner?" Perkins asked with a smirk as he passed me on his way out the door.

"Fine," I grumbled.

Lint hung up the phone and looked up at me with a big grin. "Mornin', bud," he said.

Ugh. Now we're buds. "Morning," I returned.

"That was Detective Grace on the phone," Lint informed me. "He said they put a detail on the Wilkes'. He also said they both tried to deny any involvement with the swingers club."

"You do not talk about Sex Club—that's rule number three," I stated. I stowed my weapon and sat down at my desk. I unwrapped a peanut butter cup and tossed it into my mouth, then grabbed another one and threw it on Lint's desk.

"Thanks," he said, and laid it aside. "Mr. and Mrs. Wilkes made out a list of club members. Grace is gonna fax it over. He said most of the names are Wilmington residents with the exception of the Truitts and another couple over in Little River."

I got back up from my desk and went to the coffee maker. I poured myself a cup and then offered one to Lint.

"Sure," he said.

I picked up a jelly bun and bit into it, the jelly dripped onto the front of my shirt. Goddammit!

"Ha!" Lint chuckled. "They go right to your belly, don't they?"

"Yeah." I grabbed a napkin and did my best to wipe away the glob; it left a huge stain I would have to live with for the rest of the day. "Donut?" I asked.

"No, thanks. Bertie made me breakfast this morning."

I walked back to my chair. "Let me guess, tofu and eggs with a side of ice chips."

"No, just sausage and eggs."

I let out a loud sigh and opened the bottom drawer in my desk in search of the forms I needed to start the paperwork caused by my double date with Lint. "Well, better get started on this—"

Merle's door swung open. "Here ya go," he said, walking over and handing a folder to Lint. "Thanks for getting that paperwork done so quickly, Lint." He threw me a look. "Some of these other guys could learn a thing or two from you."

"Thanks, Cap'n," Lint beamed.

Merle returned to his office and Lint tossed the folder on my desk. "Can you give these a look and sign them?"

"What is it?" I asked.

"The paperwork from last night's robbery."

"You wrote it up already?"

"Yeah, I figured I might as well get it out of the way early."

"What time did you get here?"

"Six-thirty."

I wondered exactly how many Reese's Peanut Butter Cups I would have to force feed him to revive the *old* Lint. The new Lint was really starting to piss me off.

Chapter Nineteen

The other name on the list Detective Grace had sent was Roseman: Lester and Vivian. From the looks of their home on Hermitage Drive, they were just as wealthy as the Lindell's.

"Must be a pretty elite group," Lint commented as we pulled up.

"I guess you have to be rich to be a swinger," I responded.

Lint laughed. "I would imagine they have swingers clubs for poor people too, but would you really want to join? Seems like it might be kind of nasty."

"I guess I'll just have to wait till I hit the lottery before Bree and I go swinging."

We climbed out of the car and walked up the rose-lined concrete pathway that led to the Rosemans' front door. I rung the bell and reached for my shield.

A woman probably in her mid-fifties answered the door; she was about five-three. Her face was spray-tanned to match an orange construction cone' and her short blonde haircut looked more like the feathers on a chickens ass than human hair.

"Mrs. Roseman?" I asked, showing my badge.

She cocked her head. "Yes. Can I help you?"

"I'm Detective Stellar and this is Detective Lint, we're with the North Myrtle Beach Police Department. We were wondering if we could come in and ask you a few questions."

She pulled reading glasses from her breast pocket, slid them on her nose, and took a second to read our IDs. "I already spoke on the phone with a detective this morning," she informed us. "A Detective Grace, I think it was."

"Yes, ma'am, he's with the Wilmington Police Department. We're working on the same case."

"I told the detective we didn't know anything."

Mrs. Roseman we know you're in the same, uh … club as two of the victims," I said.

"We're in no club."

She tried to close the door so I wedged my foot between the door and the jamb. "Mrs. Roseman we wouldn't make these accusations if we didn't have proof."

"Please remove your foot."

Lint spoke up. "Ma'am, we're trying to keep you and your husband's names out of the press but we may find that impossible without your help."

She released her grip on the door. "Why would our names be in the paper?" she asked.

We both stared at her in silence.

"So you're blackmailing us," she said.

"We're trying to help you," I said. "Can we come in?"

She pulled open the door, gave us the fakest of smiles, and said, "Yes, please, come in."

"Thank you," I said.

We followed her through the foyer and down a hallway. She stopped and turned when she reached the entrance to the living room. She probably referred to it as a parlor or perhaps a sitting room, for no other reason than the fact that she was wealthy.

"Have a seat," she said. "Mr. Roseman is in the backyard. I'll go get him."

Lint and I sat in matching chairs, with a small end table between us. A Tiffany lamp worth more than my truck sat on the table. Our backs were to a large window that looked out onto Hermitage Drive. Across the room from us was a sofa that matched the chairs. A glass coffee table with brass legs sat between us and the sofa. The egg and dart crown molding, painted antique white, was a classy touch, but the floral wallpaper was loud and garish, reminding me of a nineteenth century whorehouse. A brick masonry fireplace, soaring as high as the vaulted ceiling, dominated the wall. I stared in fascination at a fat, naked cupid eternally pissing into a koi-filled mini-pond—proof that shitloads of money can't buy good taste.

"Bree ever refer to you as *Mr.* Stellar?" Lint asked as he gawked at the room.

"No. It's usually just Jake ... or asshole," I replied.

"How much you think a house like this goes for?"

"I don't know, a million maybe. More than my house, that's for sure."

"Bertie's too."

"Bertie doesn't look like she hurting any."

Lint nodded in agreement. "Yeah. I wonder what she's worth."

"She hasn't told you?"

"No, and I haven't mentioned it. All she says is that her late husband left her with nothing to worry about."

"So, I guess you probably don't have anything to worry about now either."

Lint gave a sly grin. "Not if I play my cards right."

Mr. and Mrs, Roseman walked into the room; we both stood.

Distinguished, silver-haired Lester Roseman looked like an actor perfect for playing the head of a high-powered law firm in a cheesy made for TV movie. His square jaw, broad shoulders, and piercing, steel-blue eyes screamed *I'm the most important man in the room, ladies and gentlemen.*

"Detective Jake Stellar," I said extending my hand. Lint introduced himself and did the same.

Roseman looked at our hands as though we hadn't washed them in a week. He glanced at his wife and then back at me.

"What can I do for you, Detective?" Roseman asked.

I dropped my arm to my side. "We're investigating three murders, Mr. Roseman, two in Wilmington and the other in North Myrtle Beach."

He stared at us blankly. "And I repeat: What can *I* do for you?"

Lint spoke. "We understand you and your wife are members of the same, uh, exclusive social club as the three victims."

Roseman folded his arms across his chest. "I'm afraid I don't know what you're talking about, Detective."

"We're talking about the sex club you belong to," Lint explained. He was losing his cool. "The one where you meet at different club members' homes and fuck each other's wives."

Mrs. Roseman gasped. "Well, I never!" she exclaimed.

"I highly doubt that, sister," Lint shot back.

His blunt description of the swingers club caught me a little off guard too, but I tried my best not to show it.

"I'm gonna have to ask you to leave," Roseman said.

Lint spun on his heels and started back toward the front door. "That's fine, Roseman," he said. "I'll be sure to mention your name and how helpful you were at this afternoon's press conference."

"Hold on," I said. "Let's everyone calm down." Lint halted and turned back toward us. "Mr. Roseman, I'm sure you don't want your name connected to this. All we're asking is that you answer a few questions. We know you were part of this club—your name was given to us by other members, and the Wilmington PD has you on surveillance arriving at one of the parties held by the Conner's."

Roseman looked at his wife; she provided no answers, if that's what he was looking for. He cleared his throat and scratched his head. "We've only been members for a short time," he admitted in a soft, defeated voice "And we've only attended three meetings. We decided it wasn't for us."

"We were just looking for something to spice things up," Mrs. Roseman added.

Lint walked quietly back into the room.

"Two of the three members that were murdered had recently cheated on their spouse outside the club," I said.

127

"That's not permitted," said Mrs. Roseman.

"We know about the rules," Lint informed her.

"Do you think that's why they were murdered?" Roseman asked. He was staring at the floor.

"We're not sure," I said. "But we would like to put a unit outside your home until we have more answers."

The Roseman's looked at each other. "This is so embarrassing," Mrs. Roseman said.

"The same two members met their dates at the same hotel, The Castaway Beach Inn on Ocean Boulevard," I said. "Have either one of you ever stayed there?"

They both shook their heads no.

"We would like you to make a list of the members of the club, just to see if the others left anyone off of the lists they made." I glanced over at Lint; he removed his notepad and pen from his pocket.

"Here," Lint said, flipping the pad to an empty page and handing it to Roseman. "You can write the names on this."

Roseman took the pad, handed it to his wife, and then began reciting names. "There's the Lindells, of course, and the Wilkes." He scratched his chin. "Oh, and the Truitts ... and their friends. Is there anyone else honey?"

Mrs. Roseman sat on the couch with the pen in her hand looking like a kid taking a test she hadn't studied for. "I can't think of anyone else, honey" she said.

Roseman held out his hand and his wife handed him the notepad. He turned and handed it to Lint.

"Thank you," said Lint.

"Was there anyone in the group that didn't get along?" I asked. "Did you ever witness an argument between any of the members?"

"No," Roseman stated. "Not that I can remember. Everyone always seemed to have a really good time."

"Believe me when I tell you," I informed them, "I feel just as awkward asking these questions as you do answering them, but what exactly went on at these meetings? What did you do … besides the obvious?"

The Rosemans exchanged another meaningful glance. As semi-sleazy as they were, I figured they shared the same kind of spousal telepathy as Bree and me.

Mr. Roseman said, "We would sit by the pool. Conner would cook something on the grill. His wife would serve drinks. We listened to music. After a few hours we would pair off and go up to the bedrooms."

"How did you know who you were supposed to pair up with?" Lint asked.

"You would just get a look," Mrs. Roseman explained. "You know, you would catch one of the men staring at you, and you just knew."

"And one time we had a key party," Roseman said. "Everybody dropped their car keys into a bowl. The women reached into the bowl and whoever's keys they pulled out, that was their partner for the evening."

"No one got stuck with somebody they didn't want?" I asked.

"Someone ugly," Lint added.

Mrs. Roseman smiled. "Most everyone was attractive."

"But never an argument?" I asked again.

"No," said Mrs. Roseman.

"Well, there was that one time" Roseman said, pointing his finger at nothing in particular. Mrs. Roseman looked at her husband with her head cocked. "You remember, the guy that tried to crash the party the second time we were there."

"Oh, that's right," Mrs. Roseman said. "Conner and Parry wouldn't let him in. They told him he had to leave."

"Who was the man?" I asked.

Mrs. Roseman shrugged her bony shoulders. "I don't know his name. We had never met him."

"Why wasn't he allowed to stay?" Lint asked.

"Parry said he couldn't come alone," Mrs. Roseman replied. "She told him, 'Those are the rules.'"

"What made him think he could just show up like that? Was he invited?" Lint asked.

Roseman said, "I asked Conner about it later. He told me that the guy's wife had passed away a few months earlier, that they had been members, but with his wife gone he couldn't just show up stag."

Mrs. Roseman jumped in. "The whole time they argued at the gate, Parry kept saying, 'Those are the rules, those are the rules,' over and over again."

"And then the man left?" I asked.

"Yes," Roseman answered. "But he was very upset."

Lint and I looked at each other. "But you can't remember his name?" I asked.

"No one ever said his name," said Roseman.

I stood and something out the window caught my eye—a patrol car. It pulled up across the street and parked.

"The unit is here to watch the house," I informed the Rosemans. "If you need anything, don't hesitate to ask one of the officers." I pulled my business card from the inside pocket of my jacket and handed it to Mr. Roseman. "If you think of anything else please, give me a call. My cell number is at the bottom."

"Thank you," Roseman said, and then we thanked both of them for their cooperation.

On the way down the path to the street Lint and I exchanged nods with the two officer's in the squad car, they nodded back.

"Do you think they're in any real danger?" Lint asked.

"Probably not," I replied. "If the guy who tried to crash the party is our guy, he probably didn't even know them."

"I didn't know Wilmington PD had the Rosemans on video at the Lindells' house."

"They don't. I lied."

As we pulled away from the curb Lint said, "From now on, when you guys come up to the camp, we will not be tossing our car keys into that bowl by the front door."

"Way ahead of ya," I said.

Chapter Twenty

On our way back to the station, Lint phoned Detective Grace to fill him in on the man who tried unsuccessfully to attend the sex party. He told Grace we would question Marnie Truitt about it. Grace said he and Lynch would take a ride over to the Wilkes' home to see if they could shed any light on the incident.

Lint also called Marnie Truitt. Her phone went right to voicemail, so he left a message for her to call one of us. Then he phoned Brock Carmichael; no answer there either.

"You hungry?" Lint asked when he hung up his phone.

He may not be eating the large portions he used to eat, but he still thinks about food constantly. I'll break him. It's only a matter of time.

"I could eat," I replied. "Where would you like to go?" I figured I would let him pick the place for a change. Maybe being in one of his favorite eateries would be just the nudge he needed to fall off the diet wagon.

"Keep on Seventeen," Lint directed. "There's a place up here I've been wanting to try."

I bet he heard the place has great desserts, I thought.

As we drove past the Myrtle Beach Mall I pointed out that we would soon be leaving North Myrtle Beach.

"Yeah, it's right up here," Lint said.

When we reached Seventy-Sixth Avenue North, Lint said, "Turn here. And then turn into the parking lot."

I pulled into the parking lot of the Northwood Plaza Shopping Center.

Lint pointed at a sign that read Bay Naturals. "There it is."

I pulled into a parking spot facing the cafe. "Uh, what is this?"

"It's supposed to be pretty good. I guess they have a lot of healthy choices."

"Healthy choices?" I asked. "I was hoping for a burger."

"I'm sure they have burgers," Lint said as he hoisted himself out of the passenger seat.

"I didn't mean a veggie burger. Wouldn't you rather go to Sonic, or Taco Bell?"

Lint laughed. "Come on, let's try something new."

I got out of the car and followed Lint. I felt like I was in a lost episode of *The Odd Couple* in which Oscar was slowly transforming into Felix. I glanced across the parking lot at the Pet Lovers Warehouse, wishing I was eating there instead.

We grabbed a seat at a small table with two chairs. A waitress brought us a menu.

"How y'all today?" said a skinny young lady who,

like most health nuts I'd ever seen. Looked like a walking billboard for death. "My name is Ariel, and I'll be your server. I'll leave these menus and be right back."

As the young waif walked away, I commented to Lint, "You want to end up that skinny?"

Without looking up from his menu he said, "I'd like to end up that flat-chested for once in my life."

He had a point—his man boobs were larger than most women's hooters … and shapelier than some, it pains me to admit. I scanned the menu. "I don't see any soda on here. What am I supposed to drink?"

"These smoothies look good," Lint recommended. "They have iced tea, coffee, and juice."

The emaciated waitress returned. "Did you decide what you would like to drink?"

"I'll have the green peach smoothie," Lint said.

"I guess I'll have the iced tea," I said.

"Do you know what you would like to eat?" she asked.

Lint said, "I'm gonna get the veggie dog and a garden salad with balsamic vinaigrette."

I wanted to order a fork to jab in my temple, but instead ordered a tuna salad sandwich. I searched the menu for French fries, but they were nowhere to be found.

"Thank you," said Ariel cheerfully. "I'll be back with those in a bit."

I gazed around the room and my eyes stopped on a banner hanging from the ceiling that read BAY NATURALS—HEALTHY LIVING STARTS HERE. I hoped it ended here as well.

Not only was Bay Naturals a health food *cafe*, it was also a health food *grocery store*. I guess that was in case you finished eating and decided you would like to punish yourself at home as well.

"You know, there was spinach in that smoothie you ordered," I told Lint.

"I know, it sounded good," he replied.

I placed my elbows on the table, wove my fingers together, and rested my chin on my knuckles. "So tell me, Lint, when did drinking spinach first start sounding good to you?"

"You sound like a psychiatrist."

"That's because you sound like a crazy person."

"My father had a stroke and died at age fifty-one, Jake, and my mother died of a massive heart attack at forty-seven. They were both big like me. Thanks to Bertie, for the first time in a long time I feel like I have something to live for, something to be happy about. Why can't you be supportive?"

Well, don't I feel stupid. "So, what do you think about the guy who they wouldn't let into the party?" I asked, changing the subject.

Ariel returned with our drinks, and Lint waited until she left to speak. "I hope the Wilkes give Grace and Lynch a name."

"It's too bad sex clubs don't keep records."

"Yeah, too bad. Maybe he was just pissed about being shunned and wanted to get even."

"I can see him wanting to get even with the Lindells, but why Roger Truitt? Roger didn't make the rules, or enforce them."

"Maybe Marnie Truitt can shed some light it."

"Maybe," I agreed. "Why don't you try her cell again? I would like to talk to her this afternoon."

As Lint dialed his cell phone and listened to Marnie's ringtone, Ariel returned with our lunch.

"Here you go," said Ariel, setting our plates in front of us. "Is there anything else I can get you?"

Some real food. "I don't think so," I said.

Lint hung up his phone and said, "No, thanks." Ariel walked away from the table and Lint looked at me. "She's still not answering." He sucked a big gulp of his smoothie through the green plastic straw. "Mmm, that is good."

"I'll bet it is," I said, as I watched his reaction to the instant brain freeze.

He took a bite of his pretend hot dog. "Not bad. Eating healthy probably takes a little getting used to."

I took a bite of my tuna sandwich. Luckily it tasted just like a tuna sandwich.

"How's yours?" Lint asked.

"Yummy," I replied. "Just like mom used to make."

Just as Lint was about to take his second bite, his cell phone rang. "Hello? Yeah." He sat silently for a moment as the caller spoke, and then said, "Okay … thanks … you too." He hung up the phone.

"Who was that?" I asked.

"Detective Lynch. He and Grace spoke with Fred and Lucy Wilkes. They both said they remembered the incident after being reminded of it, but didn't know too much about the guy. They said he didn't look familiar to them, and after it happened no one really spoke about it. But Mrs. Wilkes said she thought she heard Conner Lindell call him Roger or Robert."

"So we're looking for a guy whose name may or may not be Roger or Robert, and he lost his wife in the last few months. That narrows it down."

"Mrs. Wilkes also told Grace and Lynch that she overheard two other guests mention that the guy's family was worth a lot of money and owned several businesses along The Strand."

"Maybe we should get a list of all the wealthy business owners in the area and start going door to door," I joked.

"That might take a while." Lint shoved the rest of his dog into his mouth and washed it down with frozen spinach and peaches.

I drank the last of my tea and ate the last few bite of my sandwich. Ariel returned one more time to make sure we were having a healthy experience. I assured her we were. She left the check on the table.

"I hope you're paying for this," I said.

Lint reached for his wallet. "I guess I can. You can pick the next place."

"You got that right."

Lint left the money and what he thought was a reasonable tip, and I left the remainder of the tip. I guess for Lint, getting healthy didn't coincide with becoming a more generous tipper.

On the way across the parking lot Lint commented that he would have to let Bertie know how great this place was. I decided that I would not tell Bree and just keep it my little secret.

Chapter Twenty-One

On the way back to the station I called Chavez—the department's tech guy—and asked him if there was any way to cross reference business owners in North Myrtle Beach with middle-aged men who had recently lost their spouse.

"Uh … not really," was Chavez's answer.

"That's weird," I informed him. "Because they do shit like that on *Criminal Minds* all the time and it only takes about two minutes."

Chavez laughed. "Well let me call Hollywood and see if they can do it for us."

"That's probably not in the budget."

"What I can do is search women in the area who have recently passed and then check to see if they were married, and then see if the widower owns a business. Then I can run the names to see if any of them have a criminal past. What type of business does he own?"

"We're not sure. We don't even know if he owns a

business. We were told that his family owned several businesses in the area."

"How old is he?"

"Don't know."

"What *do* you know about him?"

"He's Caucasian."

"Imagine that, a Caucasian dude in lily-white North Myrtle Beach. That really narrows it down, Jake. I'll see what I can do."

"Thanks, Chavez."

"And this will take a lot longer than two minutes." He hung up the phone.

As we passed Middle Gate Road a call came over the radio—a possible jumper at the Ocean Creek Resort.

"That's right up here," Lint said. "Let's check it out."

I hit the lights and pushed the gas pedal to the floor. When I came to Ocean Creek Drive I took a right. I brought the car to a stop in the circled driveway in front of the resort. Two police cruisers pulled in behind me.

Me, Lint, and the two officers driving the cruisers leapt from our cars and ran into the building. A bald, portly man met us halfway across the foyer; he was pointing upward and shouting, "Fourteenth floor, fourteenth floor!"

I turned to the two uniforms. "See if you can spot the jumper from the ground and get everyone away from the building. Lint and I will head up."

"I looked at the bald man. "What room?"

"Um, fourteen-oh-seven."

We ran for the elevator.

The door to room 1407 was propped open with a housekeeper's cart. We entered cautiously, not wanting to frighten anyone who might be clutching the balcony railing one hundred and forty feet above the pool.

We made our way down the hall past the bathroom and a small kitchenette. The hallway opened up into the living room. A Hispanic woman, probably mid-forties, stood just inside the sliding glass door; she was pleading with the jumper to please come back over the railing.

Lint gently grabbed the woman's shoulders and pulled backwards away from the door.

I stuck my head outside and said, "Beautiful day, isn't it?"

"Don't try to stop me!" the man shouted.

I laughed. "Stop you? Why would I stop you? This is America, buddy, people are pretty much free to do what they want."

The fifty-something jumper gave me a confused look over his shoulder. "I'll do it."

"Go ahead. I get paid either way." I stepped out onto the balcony.

"Don't come any closer!"

I stepped up to the railing and looked over. "Oh, shut up. Christ! You've used every cliché imaginable since I got here: *Don't try to stop me. Don't come any closer. I'll do it.* What's next? Oh, wait, let me guess: *I have nothing to live for.*"

"You're a real asshole, pal!" he shouted.

Lint was standing in the doorway. "You should ride around all day with him," he complained. "I just might come out there and we'll jump together."

"Like I said, I don't care if you jump or not," I

repeated. "But can you help me out a little before you go?"

"Help *you*? With what?"

"Can you give me your name and tell me why you're doing this. Otherwise I'll have to leave most of my paperwork blank. My captain hates that."

"Targas, Bill Targas."

I glanced down at his feet, the heels of his sneakers were barely on the edge of the balcony.

Lint pulled out his pad and pretended to take notes. "How do you spell that?" he asked.

"T-A-R-G-A-S."

"And what made you want to jump today?" I asked.

"I just have nothing to liv—"

"Ha!" I shouted. "I knew you were gonna say it." I glanced back at Lint. "They all say it."

"Fuck you!" he yelled.

I grinned big and put up my hands. "I'm sorry, I'm sorry. Really, what made you want to do this?"

"It's my wife."

"It's always the wife. What did she do, spend all your money? No, wait. You look like the type of guy who gets slapped around by his old lady. Is that what it is, she beat the shit out of you?"

"No, she never hit me," he replied angrily.

"Then what is it? What did *she* do that was so terrible that you don't want to live anymore?"

He stared down at the pool and shook his head slowly. "She fucked around on me."

"That's it?"

"What do you mean, that's it?"

"I don't know. I just thought it must have been something a lot worse. I thought somebody died or something."

"I just never thought Tammy would—"

"Whoa, wait a minute," I said. "Tammy, Tammy Targas? Your wife is Tammy Targas?"

"Yeah. Why? You know her?"

"You bet I do. I've been banging her for two years. Nice piece of tail you got there, pal."

Bill Targas looked back at me with fire in his eyes. He let go of the railing with his right hand, doubled his fist, and swung at me.

I grabbed his arm with my left and slapped on the cuffs with my right. Unbeknownst to Bill I had already secured one of the cuffs around my own wrist.

Lint dove for me just as Bill's feet slipped from the edge.

Bill's weight bent me over the railing and just as my feet left the balcony, Lint grabbed the waistband of my pants and pulled me back down.

Bill screamed as he dangled from my handcuffs. "Help me, Help me!" he shouted.

"Did you change your mind, Bill?" I hollered back.

Miraculously, Bill *had* changed his mind, so together Lint and I pulled him back up over the railing to safety. He didn't even thank Lint or me. As a matter of fact, he didn't seem to want anything to do with us even after we had saved his life. Some people are just really ungrateful.

When Lint and I walked back out to the car, they were placing Bill into the back of a squad car. We waived, but he turned his head in the other direction.

143

As the squad car pulled away I turned back toward the building. The big sign out front read, OCEAN CREEK RESORT, and underneath that, in small letters, it said, THE BRIGGS GROUP.

"Well, son of a bitch."

Chapter Twenty-Two

In a rare display of benevolence, I finally let Lint drive the Charger. All that horsepower went to his head … or rather to his foot, which was made of lead. Now I knew how Spritle and Chim Chim must have felt when they stowed away in the Mach 5. As we sped along North Kings Highway with the lights flashing, I dialed Wally Crane.

"Yeah?" Wally answered.

"Wally, it's Detective Stellar."

"What's up, dude?"

"Where are you?"

"Home."

"Your manager at the hotel, Ron Briggs—did his wife recently pass away?"

"Yeah, dude. Cancer. Very sad."

"Is Briggs working today?"

"I don't know, man."

I hung up, got on the radio, and called for backup at the Castaway Beach Inn and the Ocean Bay Club.

When Lint swung a hard right onto Twenty-First Avenue, I saw my life flash before my eyes.

"Easy there, Lint!" I said after I'd picked my heart up off the floorboard.

"Sorry. I'm channeling my inner Speed Racer."

"Yeah, well, this isn't a cartoon. If we crash, we won't turn into human accordions—we'll be dead. Savvy?"

"Roger that."

I called Marnie Truitt; still no answer.

Lint brought the car to a halt in front of The Castaway. Two units pulled up at the same time.

I shoved open the door and jumped from the car. "Block this street and keep everyone away from the front of this building!" I shouted. I pulled my 9mm.

Two of the officers climbed back in their cruisers and positioned them across the street to stop traffic. The other two began herding pedestrians away from the hotel.

Weapons drawn, Lint and I made our way cautiously to the front door. Lint pulled it open and I entered first. The same short fat lady was behind the counter.

"Where's Ron Briggs?" I asked.

She was startled. "He … he's not here today."

"Do you know where he is?"

She shook her head no. "He said he had some things to take care of."

My cell phone rang. The caller ID said Marnie Truitt. "Marnie," I said. "Where are you?"

"At the condo. Why, is something wrong?"

"Do you know a man by the name of Ron Briggs?"

"Yes. We've known him for a few years. Hold on, Jake someone's at the door."

"Marnie! Don't answer the door!" I shouted into the phone.

She must have taken the phone away from her ear. I heard her call out, "Brock, can you get the door please."

"No, don't answer the door. God dammit!"

Then there was a loud pop and Marnie screamed, "Brock!"

"Marnie!" I shouted, and ran out of the office and toward the car. Lint was right behind me.

I ran with the phone to my ear.

Marnie screamed my name and then the phone went silent.

*****

There were three other units at the Ocean Bay Club when we arrived; two were in the street blocking traffic, and the third sat at the entrance to the parking garage. All of their light bars were flashing and a crowd was beginning to gather.

"Secure a one block perimeter around this building!" I shouted to one of the officers. "I don't want anyone near this place."

"Yes, sir," one of them hollered back.

Lint and I ran into the building and straight to the

elevator. When we reached the twelfth floor the doors parted and we were met by two uniforms.

"What do we got?" I asked.

"We're not sure," one of the officers replied. "We heard some shouting when we first arrived, but—"

The other officer jumped in. "We heard a male voice shout, 'I've got a gun. Anyone comes through that door and I kill them all.'"

"That doesn't sound good," Lint said.

"Are the adjoining condos evacuated?" I asked.

"Yes, and the ones below and above," one said.

The other added, "The occupants are down a few floors in a common room. Pierce is with them."

"Good." We walked out onto the walkway and toward room 1209. Officer Pat Murray stood to the left of the door, a twelve gauge pump action shotgun balanced across his forearm.

"What's the matter, Pat, they won't let you in?" Lint asked.

"I was just trying to spread the good word about our lord and savior," said Pat, breaking the tension with welcome gallows humor.

I put my back to the wall to the left of the door and pounded on it with my fist. "Ron Briggs," I yelled. "It's Detective Stellar. You think you could unlock this door?"

Briggs fired a round through the door, hitting the walkway railing. The ricochet sounded like an old TV Western. Everyone flinched.

"Jesus Christ!" Lint said. "Didn't see that coming."

"Come on," I said to Lint. I pushed open the door to 1208 and we went inside.

"What do you have in mind?" Lint asked as we made our way down the hall to the living room and to the sliding glass door that led to the balcony.

I quietly slid open the glass door and stepped out onto the balcony. "You think I can jump from this balcony to that one?" I asked.

"Lint looked over the railing. "Well, yeah, it's only about four feet, but it's gotta be a hundred and fifty foot drop … I mean, if you drop."

"I don't plan on dropping." I leaned over the edge to get a better look. There were two sliders exiting onto the balcony; one to the living room, and the other to the master bedroom. I could see Briggs, his back was to the slider. I looked down at the pool below. The only person down there was the officer who had cleared the area.

"You want me to call Briggs' attention to the front door while you do this?" Lint asked.

"You think you can bust through that steel door if you have to?" I asked.

Lint nodded. "That's a big 10-4. I'm still fat enough to do that."

I grinned. "Tell Pat to get out here with that shotgun. You keep talking to Briggs through the front door. Be careful, he might fire again."

"You got it," Lint said, and walked back through the slider.

A few seconds later Pat Murray walked onto the balcony carrying the shotgun.

"What's the plan?" Pat asked.

"I'm going to climb over to that other balcony—"

"You sure you want to do that?"

"It's only about four feet."

"It's a hell of a lot more than four feet *down*," Pat argued.

"When I nod my head I want you to fire that shot gun through the farthest slider over."

"You're the boss," Pat said and pumped the shotgun.

As I climbed over the railing I could hear Lint hollering to Briggs. He was telling Briggs to answer Marnie Truitt's cell phone. Pat took aim at the glass.

I stood with my ass to the railing and my heels on the balcony ledge. I took a deep breath and leaped. Fear made me over-compensate for the distance and I slammed both knees against the steel spindles of the other railing; it sounded like a gong. I jumped over the railing and moved closer to the slider that led to the master bedroom.

I turned back and nodded to Pat. He fired, shattering the sliding glass door. I pulled open the other door and went inside. I could hear Marnie's phone ringing.

"Can I answer it?" I heard Marnie ask.

"I said no!" Briggs hollered. Then I heard the smack of his hand against Marnie's face. She cried out.

I waited for Lint to yell again and then I pulled the door open a crack. Briggs was standing behind Marnie; he had his left arm around her throat and a pistol in his right hand. I couldn't see Brock or Bambi Carmichael.

I stepped into the living room, my 9mm trained on Briggs' forehead. "Drop that weapon, Briggs," I said.

He tightened his grip and spun around, placing Marnie between him and me. He jammed the gun into her ribs. "I'll kill her!" he shouted.

"I know," I said.

Briggs began backing up toward the balcony.

"Drop the gun," I ordered.

"You don't make the rules here, Stellar. I'm making the rules now." He put his mouth next to Marnie's ear. "We gotta play by the rules, don't we, Marnie?"

I kept my weapon aimed at Briggs' head. "It wasn't Marnie that made you follow the rules, Briggs, it was the Lindell's."

"No, but she broke the rules when she screwed Carmichael at my hotel. Now she's gotta pay. They all made me follow the rules, but they didn't follow them."

"I know, Briggs, but this isn't the way to do it."

"My wife died. I had nobody. They wouldn't even talk to me anymore. They wouldn't let me come to the parties. 'It's the rules, Ron, it's the rules,' that bitch kept saying. I showed her who makes the rules."

Briggs stepped back over the threshold onto the balcony, the broken glass crunching beneath his feet. He pulled Marnie with him. He caught a glimpse of Pat Murray and turned his head.

Marnie bit Briggs' arm as hard as she could and then dropped to the floor.

Briggs screamed and raised his weapon.

I fired three rounds into his chest, knocking him backwards over the railing. I glanced behind me. Brock Carmichael lay on his back in the hall. Enough blood had pooled on the floor that I knew he was dead the moment I saw him.

"Where's Bambi?" I asked.

"In the bathroom," Marnie replied. "He didn't hurt her."

I walked past Marnie onto the balcony and peered over the rail. Briggs was floating on his back in the pool, the water around him slowly turning red.

Marnie sat in the shattered glass sobbing.

I looked over to the next balcony, Lint and Pat were also gazing over the railing.

"You okay?" Lint asked.

"I'm fine," I answered.

The officer standing next to the pool now had his hands on his hips and was looking up at us.

Lint cupped his hands around his mouth and shouted down, "Hey, can you grab a net? There's some crud floating in the pool."

Me and Pat just shook our heads.

The End

Coming Soon

Deadly Moves
From the Tales of Dan Coast

and

Sunrise City

ALSO BY RODNEY RIESEL

Sleeping Dogs Lie
From the Tales of Dan Coast

A mystery set in the Florida Keys follows Dan Coast, an unlicensed private detective of sorts, as he is hired to find the missing boyfriend of a woman who herself soon ends up missing. When someone from the woman's past unexpectedly shows up at Dan's home, with a story of faked deaths and missing life insurance money; Dan along with his sidekick Red set out to find the money, and the woman.

ISBN: 978-0-9883503-0-4

Ocean Floors
From the Tales of Dan Coast

The second installment in the Dan Coast series, Ocean Floors, is a tale of mystery and possible romance when a chance meeting with a beautiful young woman leads Dan and his trusted sidekick Red down a road of murder and kidnapping. Join Dan and Red as they try to solve the murder while searching for a missing friend.

ISBN: 978-0-9894877-0-2

North Murder Beach
A Jake Stellar Novel

The first installment of the story of North Myrtle Beach police detective, Jake Stellar. The spring bike rallies have ended, the spring breakers have all gone back to school, and the summer tourist season is a few weeks away. What better time for a police officer to take a nice quiet relaxing week off from work? That's what Jake Stellar had in mind. That is until someone from his past resurfaces to remind him of a terrible secret he has spent years trying to forget. In North Murder Beach, a story of revenge, Jake is unwillingly and violently forced to confront his secret from his past.

ISBN: 978-0-9894877-1-9

The Coast of Christmas Past
From the Tales of Dan Coast

Coast of Christmas Past is the third book in the Dan Coast series of books. Dan Coast is all set to spend Christmas just the same way he has every year for the past few years; alone and drunk. But when uninvited, unexpected guests arrive and throw a wrench into his holiday plans he is forced to sober up (slightly), and throw on a smile. Just when it seems nothing else could go wrong, a close friend is injured in what appears, to the police, to be a drug deal gone bad. Dan Coast and his sidekick, Red jump into action to find the truth while their friend lies unconscious in the hospital.

ISBN: 978-0-9894877-3-3

The Man in Room Number Four
The Dunquin Cove Series

When a mysterious stranger arrives in the small coastal town of Dunquin Cove, Maine it appears as though Claire and her young son, Mica's prayers have been answer.

But who is he, and why is he really here? Join Claire and her guests at the Colsome House Bed and Breakfast as they piece together the mystery of the Man in Room Number Four.

ISBN: 978-0-9894877-2-6

Ship of Fools
From the Tales of Dan Coast

Ship of Fools is the fourth book in The Tales of Dan Coast series and begins where Coasts of Christmas Past left off. Find out how Dan deals with the death of a young friend, while looking into the disappearance of a new friend's sister. Join Dan, Red, and Skip as they fumble their way through a new mystery.

ISBN: 978-0-9894877-4-0

Beach Shoot
A Jake Stellar Series

It's a beautiful Sunday morning in North Myrtle Beach and Emily Bowen, a wife and mother of four, lies dying on the beach. Jake Stellar returns in Beach Shoot, a new mystery by Rodney Riesel.

Beach Shoot is the second Jake Stellar book and sequel to the Amazon Best Seller North Murder Beach. In Beach Shoot, Jake finds himself teamed up with the most unlikely of partners, his nemesis and fellow detective Avis Lint. Join Jake and Avis as they piece together the clues in this thrilling new mystery.

ISBN: 978-0-9894877-5-7

Return to Dunquin Cove
The Dunquin Cove Series

It's been almost six months since the day ex-hitman, Ben Dunning turned up in Dunquin Cove, Maine, not knowing where or who he was. He's lived a quiet, peaceful life in the small town, but now his old life is calling him back. As Ben plans a trip to Boston in search of his past, little does he know that trouble is brewing in Dunquin Cove. Two strangers have arrived with the promise of safety and security. Join Ben and the people of Dunquin Cove as they band together to prove they can take care of themselves and their town.

ISBN: 978-0-9894877-7-1

Double Trouble
From the Tales of Dan Coast

Shortly after Walter and Warren Bowman arrive in Key West in search of a sister they never knew they had, Warren disappears. With nowhere else to turn, Walter enlists the help of Dan Coast. Join Dan as he and sidekick Red Baxter search for the missing Bowman family members, while dealing with the fallout of an ongoing case.

ISBN: 978-0-9894877-9-5

When Death Returns
A Jake Stellar Series

Has a serial killer from the past returned to North Myrtle Beach? Jake Stellar is back in When Death Returns. Join Jake and his partner Avis Lint in this exciting third installment of the Jake Stellar series as they investigate a homicide that eerily echoes the past.

ISBN: 978-0-9971149-0-4

From Here to There: A Collection of Short Stories

Within this book is a collection of short stories I have written over the past few years. The stories were mostly inspired by trips I've taken, places I've stayed, and conversations I've overheard from Maine to Florida. Although these stories differ from ones I have released in the past, I hope you will enjoy reading them as much as I enjoyed writing them.

ISBN: 978-0-9971149-1-1

Most Likely to Die
From the Tales of Dan Coast

How does someone with no enemies end up murdered? That's for Dan Coast and his sidekick Red Baxter to find out. Join Dan and Red, along with Skip Stoner and Dan's childhood hero, former astronaut, Kip Larson as they piece together the clues that may free an innocent man. In this action packed, sixth installment of The Tales of Dan Coast Series, Dan digs into a wrongly accused man's past and finds out he may not be so innocent.

ISBN: 978-0-9971149-2-8